"Bends me on when you all tough on me," he said and stepped forward.

He could run from the stunning strength of his attractit do? He'd had ow how to have f Although the from ideal, it distraction ra with the mission.

He made a decision in that moment. The next, she was snugly enfolded in his arms.

Her eyes went wide and for a moment he felt as if he could fall into those golden pools. Then he reminded himself that agents didn't fail.

So he moved ahead and conquered.

Intimate Details
DANA MARTON

MILLS & BOON®
Pure reading pleasure

First published in Great Britain 2008
by Harlequin Mills & Boon Limited,
Eton House, 18-24 Paradise Road, Richmond, Surrey TW9 1SR

© Marta Dana 2007

ISBN: 978 0 263 85969 0

46-0608

Harlequin Mills & Boon policy is to use papers that are
natural, renewable and recyclable products and made from
wood grown in sustainable forests. The logging and
manufacturing processes conform to the legal environmental
regulations of the country of origin.

Printed and bound in Spain
by Litografia Rosés S.A., Barcelona

With many thanks to Denise Zaza and
Allison Lyons for taking a chance on the
MISSION: REDEMPTION books.

DANA MARTON

lives near Wilmington, Delaware. She has been
an avid reader since childhood and has a master's
degree in writing popular fiction. When not
writing, she can be found either in her garden
or her home library. For more information on
the author and her other novels, please visit her
website at www.danamarton.com.

She would love to hear from her readers via email:
DanaMarton@yahoo.com.

CAST OF CHARACTERS

Gina Torno – She hadn't forgiven herself for the crime that had landed her in prison. Now, in the midst of mortal danger, she had to learn to trust herself...and the mysterious stranger who steals her heart with every glance.

Cal Spencer – Although not a trained operative, he finds himself in the eye of the storm, pitched against terrorists. Telling friend from foe is a challenge, especially when he meets Gina. Can he trust her enough to forge an uneasy alliance?

Carly Jones, **Samantha Hanley** and **Anita Caballo** – The other three members of Gina's team.

Brant Law – The FBI agent in charge of the four women and their mission.

Tsernyakov – The illegal weapons trader is among the top-five most wanted criminals in the world...and the team's number one target.

Mark – Tsernyakov's right-hand man on the island. His job is to secure the site and make sure that any threats to his boss are eliminated.

Prologue

"We have two weeks before we have a major terrorist attack on our hands," Brant Law, the FBI agent who had organized the mission, said over the phone. "And we don't know the location or what kind of weapon we are facing."

The mood at Savall, Ltd.'s office was somber, in stark contrast to the world outside their windows—Grand Cayman Island vacation paradise where tourists strolled the streets, letting go of the stress piled on by their corporate jobs back home, enjoying the island's perfect climate and light-hearted atmosphere.

None of them knew how quickly all that carefree mood could be erased. The small team inside the office, however, was well aware of it.

"I think there's a good chance the weapon might be on the island," Gina Torno said, wanting to inject something positive. "We might be able to find it before it changes hands."

She was referring to some mystery private island in French Polynesia they knew next to nothing about.

Joseph Towers, an enigmatic businessman, had sent the four women of Savall, Ltd. plane tickets to Acapulco. His yacht would pick them up there and take them the rest of the way—to discuss business, supposedly.

They had reason to believe, though no confirmation, that Joseph Towers was an alias for Tsernyakov, one of the biggest illegal-weapons traders in the world, a man at the top of the FBI's most-wanted list, hunted by every major law enforcement agency around the world.

"How sure are we that Joseph Towers is our T?" T was their code name for Tsernyakov. They never referred to the man by name over the phone. "We don't have time to go down the wrong path," Anita Caballo said and began to pace.

"Pretty sure," Nick Tarasov, the commando guy who had trained them, spoke up.

"The distance between pretty sure and sure is as big as between dead and almost dead," David Moretti, the team's lawyer who had orchestrated their release from Brighton FCI, remarked.

"In my line of work, sometimes it's smarter to

rely on instincts than on supposed facts," Nick shot back, the frustration in his voice unmistakable even over the phone.

They were all tense, desperate to find a way to head off disaster.

Brant, Nick and David were off-site, participating via teleconference, as always these days. They could no longer afford face-to-face contact with the all-woman team for fear that they might be watched.

The time was near. They'd uncovered a date—November twenty-seventh—that had been confirmed by independent intelligence. The date and that some serious WMD was changing hands on the black market.

"The island seems like a good place to conduct other business besides whatever he has in mind for us," Carly Jones said, riffling through a stack of computer printouts. "Away from the eagle-eyed authorities."

"I'm receiving some new information here," Brant cut in, and they could hear the clicking of his keyboard. "Okay, I'm e-mailing it to everyone."

"What is it?" Gina asked, thinking how lucky they were that they had gotten even this far, that they'd been able to make a reputation in money laundering and draw the attention of Philippe Cavanaugh, an associate of Tsernyakov's, and through him the attention of the man himself.

But the private island… If they went there, they would be in T's territory, just the four women, without backup, surrounded by ruthless criminals. How long before their luck ran out? She looked around at the teammates she had come to care about over the past months. She had talked the talk and walked the walk since she'd gotten out of Brighton Federal Correctional Institute, but inside she was scared stiff that she would let her team down the way she had let her colleagues down in the PPD—Philadelphia Police Department. The way she'd let down her family and herself.

"Photo of a possible new associate of T's. The guy has been seen around T's business interests in England. We don't have a name, just a picture," Brant was saying.

"That's more than what we have on Tsernyakov." Samantha Hanley was bringing up her e-mail already. A new message blinked onto the top of the page as they watched.

Sam opened the attachment. "I know him," she said at the same time as Gina said, "Familiar."

"Who is it?" Nick asked.

Sam drew a slow breath as she considered. "Hang on. Let me think."

"You know, I think you're right. Those eyes. I know those eyes." Anita leaned closer.

Gina was trying to come up with a name as she

focused on the green-blue wonders, which were sexy and cocky and intelligent. Much like the man—very James Bondish.

And then it hit her.

She strode to her desk, reached for the ripped-out magazine cover that Sam had tacked onto her wall weeks ago. It was him, although he looked slightly different on the surveillance photos, his hair windblown as he walked along some harbor. The guy she'd made some stupid remark about.

"Your fiancé," Anita exclaimed when Gina got back with the picture.

Gina shot her a warning look. They'd been pestering her—in a lighter, girlish moment—about not believing in love at first sight. So she'd pointed at the cover of some stupid magazine and the gorgeous guy on it and said sure she did, he was the one. And regretted it ever since. The others, of course, wouldn't let it die.

"What fiancé?" Brant asked.

"A joke. Nothing. Never mind." Gina glared at the three women who were grinning at her. "Anyway, the guy we're looking for made the cover of some Chinese business magazine back in—" she searched for the pub date "—July."

"So what's his name?"

"We don't know. It's in Chinese," Carly said.

"What's the magazine?"

The women looked at each other. Anita was the one who spoke. "That's in Chinese, too."

"For heaven's sake," Brant grumbled. "Just fax the damn thing over."

Chapter One

French Polynesia
One week later

Gina Torno padded barefoot toward the ocean, wearing nothing but a midnight-blue bikini, keeping an eye out for the motley staff that worked on their mysterious host's private island. The rest of her team—Carly, Anita and Sam—were all busy conducting their own recon missions. They needed to cover ground quickly, which required splitting up.

Two workmen were hammering something at the dock, wearing jeans and nothing else, swearing up a blue streak. The yacht that had brought the women in the night before from Acapulco was still there, as were two motorboats. The water was the most brilliant azure. Unlike Seven Mile Beach, which they had left behind on Grand Cayman, where tourists stirred up the sand.

The contrast between the gorgeous, unspoiled environment and the evil-hearted man who owned it was startling. *If* their mysterious host was Tsernyakov. They'd been hunting for the man for months now, and he proved to be as elusive as the morning mist over the ocean.

Was it possible they had him finally? Were they in time to stop a tragedy? Was he even now on the island? They'd been told that Joseph Towers was delayed on the mainland on business. But if he were Tsernyakov, they could hardly expect him to play it straight. He could be anywhere. Even here, watching them.

The staff studiously avoided any questions about him, always busy with one construction project or another. An early-season cyclone had brushed the island a few days ago and taken down some trees and rooftops.

She came upon two men sitting on a pile of coconut palms that had been twisted out by the wind.

"How are you doing?"

"Hello."

They had been deep in conversation and went back to it once she passed them. Doctors from California, here on their own business—whatever that was. They'd been introduced last night when her team had arrived.

Gina came to a fork in the path and continued

in the direction of the utility building instead of the beach. She came around a handful of coconut palms that were still standing and got an unobstructed view of the structure. A Slavic-looking guy was replacing a broken window in the front.

"Are you looking for someone?" He stopped what he was doing. Tall, blond and muscular, he sported the same island tan everybody else did. He had the same alert vigilance as the others, as if they—down to the last handyman—were all moonlighting on some security task force.

She smiled the clueless-tourist smile. "I don't suppose you've seen three women go this way? My friends. We just got here last night. This place is huge." She looked around bewildered.

"I've only been out here for a few minutes," the guy said, focusing on her cleavage.

"Thanks." She smiled again and kept walking, having no idea what to do next or where the path led. She put one foot in front of the other until she was out of sight, then moved off into the jumble of flowering bushes and doubled back, ignoring the stones and sharp bark she had to walk over now that she was off the paved path. She watched the ground for anything that moved. God only knew what kinds of nasty creepy crawlers lived under the bushes on tropical islands. She would just as soon not meet any.

She slowed, then stopped behind the last stand of taller vegetation. There was another guy in the back, up on the roof, dragging palm-frond thatching into place. Looked as though the wind had hit the building from that end and swirled the back of the roof.

She squatted out of sight and waited.

Her team's first task upon arriving on the island was twofold: to map the place and to figure out where Tsernyakov was hiding if he was here, which meant they had to comb through every building. Once they had confirmation that he was on location, they would call in the cavalry. Then they would stay out of the way while the FBI did their job.

The task seemed easy enough, except that, suspiciously, none of their cell phones seemed to work on the island. Until they figured something out, they were cut off from potential backup.

She'd liked Grand Cayman, but this island gave her the creeps. There were too many people—supposedly support staff—who were always watching. And, sure, the beach looked idyllic—all pink sand and rustic bungalows—but when they'd come in last night, she'd looked out the cabin window a few times and seen different buildings on the other side of the island. Square and stocky, without windows, they'd looked like otherworldly bomb shelters in the moonlight.

The roofer patted the palm fronds into place, then jumped to the ground and disappeared around the building. He left his tools, which meant he would be coming back. Gina stole up to the corner and peeked around it. Window guy was still there. She went to the other side. Bingo. Another broken window, about two feet by two feet. Large enough to fit through, perhaps. Looked as if most of the broken glass had been beaten out, but a few jagged edges still stuck out from the frame.

She sneaked up to it and looked inside. The room, some sort of an office, seemed deserted. Chunks of glass lay on the windowsill. The window opened in, but the edge of a cabinet was in the way. There was enough room for the window to be opened to let in some fresh air if someone wished but not enough for her to squeeze through.

Only one way to get inside.

She backed up all the way to the bushes, glanced around, then ran for it. One, two, three. Hands pointed in front, she sailed through the air, tucked and rolled, came to a halt inches from the door. She felt a flash of relief that she hadn't misjudged the distance. Someone would have heard if she'd crashed into the door pane.

Coach Wilson would have been proud. Her mother had insisted that all eight of her girls did something after school. Most of her sisters went for music and ballet. Maria played chess. Gina's thing had been gymnastics. She hadn't had the patience for chess and wasn't the type for a pink tutu. She was good at athletics, however. She'd even made it to a few state championships. Who knew those skills would come in handy this many years later?

She looked down to where pain burned in her side and found a six-inch scrape beading with blood. *Could have been worse.* If she had misjudged the height, she could have been gutted. She grabbed a piece of blank paper from the table and spit on it, then went to the window and wiped the drop of blood from the glass. She dabbed at her side, too, although it didn't seem necessary. The scratch was fairly superficial and had stopped bleeding already.

She balled the paper and tossed it into the bushes where she'd been hiding a minute ago. She would get it on her way out.

"I don't know what the rush is. He ain't barely spends time here anyway," someone mumbled outside the office door.

She ducked behind a filing cabinet, knowing it would only protect her if whoever was out there didn't take more than two steps inside the room.

"What do you care? It's the job—we do it, we get paid," another man responded.

He sounded like the window guy. Was the other one the roofer?

"I don't like the island." The voice was hoarse and scratchy, as if he had a few decades of heavy smoking in his past.

"What's not to like?"

"The gang of pirates, for one," the roofer rasped.

"They don't come here."

"But you can see the lights of their ships as they pass the island at night. Givin' me nightmares."

"They have an agreement with the boss."

"Don't think the bastards wouldn't cut our throats first chance they got."

"Worry about the roof. We have to be finished and out of here in half an hour."

"Almost done."

"That fast?"

"Five more minutes. Need a hand?"

"Sure," the window guy said.

"Wanna have another beer?" Judging from the voice, they were walking away.

"When we finish." That was the last bit of conversation she caught.

A few minutes later, the guy was back to shuffling on the roof again. She moved toward the office door and tried the handle. Locked. What if she couldn't get out through there? She definitely couldn't skip out the window. The roofer would see her from above. She didn't have much time. In a few minutes the men would begin working on the broken window behind her. They would likely enter the office to do that. If she wasn't out of here by then, she'd certainly be discovered.

She was determined not to be the one who messed up the mission. She was the only one on the team with a background in law enforcement. More so than the others, she should know what she was doing. More so than the others, she deserved to be in this mess. Anita, Carly and Sam shouldn't have been in prison in the first place.

Anita had been framed; Carly's only crime was being too intelligent for the rest of the world to know what to do with her; Sam was the product of the system that had let her down.

Her own incarceration, however, Gina thought, was fully justified. She had taken a life. And it didn't matter that she had served time to pay for that. In her own mind, it would be a long way before she was forgiven.

Maybe if the mission succeeded. If she saved all those lives at risk. Maybe that would balance the scales.

She took a few pictures with her camera ring as she shuffled through the papers on the desk—a bunch of bills, lists of building materials and supplies. None of it looked superimportant, but she didn't have time to analyze the data right now. Once she was back with the others, they could talk it over and see if they could come up with some connections, unearth some clues.

She tried the drawers, but they were locked, as were the file cabinets. She didn't dare turn on the computer. It was likely password-protected anyway. And the men might be here before the log-in screen ever came up.

Talking of the devil, there they were already.

"Nasty," the roofer said.

She squatted on the other side of the file cabinet to make sure she wouldn't be seen from the outside and prayed for a miracle.

"Want me to break out the rest of the glass?"

"Hang on. I'm going to take out the whole frame. Don't want to make a mess inside," the window guy told him.

Twenty minutes later, her knees throbbed from squatting motionless and her feet had fallen asleep, her mind numb from the crude conversation filtering in from outside. The topics centered on sex and booze, more information than she'd ever wanted to know about the special skills of some of the women who worked in the main building. And the men still weren't done with the repairs. How long did it take to change glass in a frame, anyway?

"Never saw this many guests on the island at one time," the window guy remarked.

"They could'a waited while we fixed the damn place. It stands empty months on end, and now that it's a mess, everybody's gotta be here. Maybe the boss's sellin'. Thought about that?"

"Don't be an idiot," came the annoyed response.

"He's gettin' it all fixed up, addin' a lot of stuff, too. And now he has all these people here. Maybe he'll sell off some of the houses."

Something popped.

"All right. I have to do the rest from the inside. Hold on to this and don't let it move."

No, no, no. Gina glanced around, desperate. The man couldn't come in. There was no place to hide in the small office. And even if there were, she couldn't move at all; the roofer guy outside the window would see her.

Or maybe not.

He turned to hold up the window with his back and lit a cigarette, grumbling to himself and cursing the cyclone.

She could hear the other one in the hallway. She had less than a minute.

She stepped up on the table without making a

sound, reached for the nearest ceiling panel and pushed it out of place, then pulled herself up, holding her breath so she wouldn't sneeze from the dust she was stirring up. *Oh, man.* The structure was awfully rickety up there. And pitch-dark. She didn't want to think about the inventory of tropical bugs that likely shared the space with her. She put the ceiling tile back, then spread her weight as best she could. She didn't have much time to find a comfortable spot; the door was opening below.

Somebody came in. Paused.

"Wind blew in a bunch of dust," window guy said right beneath her and moved something around on the desk. "You'll need both hands. You think you can put down that smoke for another minute or two?"

Something crawled across Gina's leg in the darkness. She shuddered. When she'd been a cop, she'd faced down deranged criminals without trouble. But the thought of palm-size tarantulas cozying up to her freaked her out. So much for the tough-chick act she'd worn since she'd signed up for the police academy then perfected on the force and polished in federal prison.

She'd been too jumpy this morning already. Stupid nightmares had come back again. Probably from the stress. Their mission was nearing its end and the stakes couldn't have been higher. She hated waking up drenched in sweat; she hated the dark swamp of guilt, the disappointment she felt in herself for having done what she'd done. The time she'd spent at Brighton should have eased her conscience, but it hadn't.

She listened to the men below and did her best to put the past out of her mind. Now wasn't the time to get distracted.

Thankfully whatever the two guys needed to do didn't take long. They were leaving within five minutes. She decided to wait another five before taking off, in case they were still cleaning up outside.

Unfortunately the door opened again before she could make her move.

"Gentlemen, please take a seat," a slightly accented voice said. It definitely didn't belong to either the window guy or the roofer, the voice more cultured, more professional. "How do you like the island so far? Sorry about the mess." Papers flapped, sounding as though he was shaking off files.

Was he wondering about the dust on his desk? Would he look up and figure out where it had come from? Gina held her breath. She'd been in tight situations before and bluffed like a pro or fought her way out if nothing else worked. But this one was stickier than the average mess-up. She would have a hard time coming up with a believable story if they caught her stuck in the ceiling. Yet panicking over the spot she was in never entered her mind. Keeping calm went a long way toward coming out of a bad situation alive.

"We're just cleaning up after the storm. Everything should be back in order within a day or two," the man said, and Gina allowed herself to relax for the moment. Didn't sound as though the guy was about to investigate the dust.

"That's fine. Doesn't look like the island was hit too badly. And it's gorgeous even with the residual damage. Thanks for having us here, Mark," someone responded.

She recognized the name. And then the voice, too, fell into place.

"And your housing?" Mark asked. As far as she could tell, he was the overseer of the island. He had greeted them in the harbor upon arrival.

"I still don't understand why we are here. There are maybe forty people on the island. You don't need two full-time doctors, not like us, anyway. There's a hospital in Papeete. I understand Mr. Towers has a helipad and an Agusta and a Bell to go with it."

So the other two were the doctors.

Gina stored the information and wondered where the helipad was and if Tsernyakov's two choppers were on the island. She didn't know much about helicopters but recognized the names of the models at least. Something else they had to investigate.

They'd been keeping an eye on the bay for arrivals from the sea. They had to get a location on the helipad, keep an ear out for any birds coming or going.

"Where is Mr. Towers?" the doctor with the deeper voice was asking.

She held her breath for the answer.

"He was held up in a meeting in Venezuela. He is expected here shortly. I have your contracts."

There was some paper crinkling below, then silence, the doctors probably skimming over what they were being offered.

Somebody cleared his throat. "What you need is a primary physician. Or even a paramedic would be sufficient. We are both specialists. Not that the offer is not generous," he rushed to add.

Gina held her breath as dust tickled her nose. Tsernyakov was bringing in two medical specialists. She would have given anything to find out what their specialties were. It might present a clue about the large-scale weapon Tsernyakov was selling, whether it was biological, chemical or a dirty bomb.

The island had a helipad and two choppers and

some serious-looking bunkers. He was beefing up staff and fixing up housing. Did that mean he planned on riding out the attack here?

"Would you at least agree to wait for Mr. Towers to discuss this with him?" Mark asked.

He sounded deceptively mild and professional. But if he was working for Tsernyakov, the doctors didn't have much of a chance. He was merely giving them the illusion that the choice was theirs. In any case, if they stayed long enough, once the attack happened, it might be impossible for them to leave.

Gina repressed a shudder, thinking of her friends and herself. What about them? If they couldn't stop the terrorist attack, would they be marooned here with Tsernyakov and his band of criminals?

Today was November twentieth. Seven more days until the red-letter day, but what was it? Was it the date for the handover of the weapon or the date for the actual attack? How were they supposed to succeed with their mission when they knew so little?

They had Philippe Cavanaugh in custody, but Cavanaugh wasn't talking. At least security had relaxed at his estate in his absence, his guards easing into complacency. The team had been successful in pulling off a night mission and gained access to both of his safes, found enough clues to confirm that Cavanaugh indeed was one of

Tsernyakov's right-hand men. Not that it was that special of a position. Tsernyakov had more right hands than the goddess Shiva.

"Of course. Spending time here is no hardship," the younger-sounding doctor said below. "I just—"

"We are probably not a good fit for the post, that's all. If Mr. Towers would like us to make a recommendation for someone who has the right skills for the type of injuries that are most likely to need treatment in a place like this, we'd be happy to help."

She turned her head in hopes of getting it out of the dust patch and stretched her arm in the process. It touched something hairy. And warm.

She bit her lip to keep from yelping. What was that? The thing didn't move. She cautiously stretched her fingers toward it again. Skin with sparse hair. A sick animal? A healthy one would have hightailed it out of here when she came up. The skin twitched. Whatever it was, it was alive. She pulled her fingers back again and tried to put the picture of a giant rat out of her mind. Not enough hair for a rat, she told herself. Still, the air caught in her lungs.

She wasn't claustrophobic, but all of a sudden it seemed there was not enough air to breathe in the small space. Every horror movie she'd ever watched came back to her with goose-bump-raising detail.

Things she could see she could take on, no matter how formidable or dangerous they seemed. The hairy thing in the dark, however, got her imagination working—and it went to places she didn't want to follow.

"You should probably read through the contract in the meanwhile, anyway. No harm in that," Mark was saying just as something closed around Gina's wrist with a sudden quick strike.

It took all her willpower not to jump, not to betray her presence to those below. Then her brain clicked back to working after the first moment of pure fright, and she registered the fingers around her wrist.

A human hand. It held her as tight as a vise.

WHO IN BLOODY HELL was that? A thief?

Cal Spencer held on to the slim wrist. A woman, for certain. The light flowery scent that emanated from the intruder's direction confirmed that.

He'd seen about a dozen female guests on the island so far, plus the five on the staff his cousin kept here.

Which one was she? What did she want?

All he wanted was for her not to blow his cover. He squeezed her wrist in a silent warning. She tugged. Not a chance. He wasn't about to let her go.

"Enjoy the beach, then. Look at this as a mini vacation," Mark was saying below them.

Chairs were shuffled, then came the sound of the door closing. Did they all leave or had Mark stayed behind to work?

The interstice where two ceiling tiles met drew Cal for a peek through, but he couldn't edge closer without letting the hand go. He tried anyway. She responded by jerking against him, hard. The structure they were suspended on trembled.

He went completely still and listened for any reaction from below.

The hellcat next to him wasn't as cautious. She kicked out, catching him in the side. He bit back a groan, then yanked her toward him. She had to be restrained before she did damage.

He felt soft naked skin, then curves as he pulled her closer. *Intriguing.* Then met the power of hard muscle as she elbowed his stomach. *Bloody hell.* He tried to put an arm around her to hold her down.

The next thing he knew, they were crashing through the ceiling in a shower of debris.

He let her go on reflex just a moment before he landed across the desk in a hard fall that could have easily snapped his back. She seemed luckier with the floor. She was on her feet before he was, breathing hard, her gold-mocha eyes throwing sparks as she rounded on him.

All right. He remembered this one—a compact, gorgeous fireball of a woman he'd been introduced to the night before. Her face was covered in dust, her sassy dark bob of hair sticking up and dusted with a bit of foam pieces, but the hot body was ID enough. Gina Torno. She was with a consulting company his cousin was interested in doing business with.

The ladies were on his list of things that needed further checking out. Looked as though he had to give them a higher priority than he had first thought. This one was definitely up to something shady.

"What are you doing here?" he asked at the same time she spit out, "Who are you?"

Since he thought she was the sexiest woman on the island, the fact that she didn't remember him from the night before stung a little. But not nearly as much as her well-aimed kick to his chin the next second.

He staggered back a few inches and stared at her, dumbfounded. How on earth did she kick that high? She was five-five at best; he was five-eleven.

"All right, that's enough, luv." He put out a placating hand and stepped closer. It seemed safest to try and grab her arms and hold them to her side while he asked some questions. And kept an eye on those legs. They were lethal.

They circled each other.

"What do you want?" she demanded.

"Ladies first." He smiled, actually enjoying the cat-and-mouse game. Hey, what guy didn't want to wrestle with a hot woman in a bikini?

Her narrowed eyes said she wasn't nearly as delighted. He caught a hint of desperation as she feinted to the right. Not bad. But not good enough to fool him. He'd been on the boxing team at Cambridge. A long time ago, granted, but some things you didn't forget.

Where had she learned her stuff? He tried to remember what he could. She was a security expert. American. Her company was based on Grand Cayman. They'd done business with one of his cousin's "friends."

"Look, let's—"

The sound of footsteps came from the hallway. Mark probably. The man had a way of being a bloody nuisance half the time. Couldn't blame him, really. It was his job to keep an eye on things on the island and make sure everything ran smoothly.

Unfortunately this objective stood in direct opposition with Cal's to search the island as thoroughly as he could and figure out a way to sabotage the plans of Mark's boss, who also happened to be Cal's second cousin. He felt a twinge of guilt as always when he thought of Joseph. He had to believe he was doing the right thing.

But still, he wished with all his heart that the SIS had been wrong about this. He could not, however, in good conscience choose to live in that fantasy. He'd seen proof and plenty of it.

The sounds from outside the door neared. Gina froze in front of the window and used her position to open it, then vault clear through before he could have gotten a clue to her intention.

He blinked. Damn, she was fast.

He stared after her, then, for the first time since they'd fallen, glanced around the destroyed room, dust and broken-up ceiling tiles everywhere. No way to make this mess disappear in the next minute.

He could follow Ms. Torno out the window, but when Mark saw this chaos there would be questions. He didn't want anyone to get suspicious and start an investigation. The last thing he needed was for security to be tightened.

He glanced up and saw a water pipe through the gaping hole above, stood on the desk and grabbed onto it, then pulled with his full weight. It bent somewhat. Then a little more. Water trickled down his arm. The next second, the pipe burst all over the place, and he slipped to the floor just as the door opened.

"Mark. Good." He was pulling the computer out of harm's way. "I just stopped by to see you. I think you had a pipe burst up there."

"I was just in here a minute ago." Mark swore and jumped to clear the papers on his desk, which were getting soaked through. Everything was now a soggy mess, quickly covering up any signs of the fight moments ago.

"When the cyclone shook the roof, it probably rattled the pipes," Mark ground out, grabbing what he could. He stopped only to yell out the door, "Turn the water main off!"

"Let me try something, mate." Cal jumped back on the desk and reached for the pipe to hold it together, reducing the water by more than half.

"Thanks," Mark said below, collecting whatever items he could salvage. "I'm glad you were here."

He searched the man's face for any sign of suspicion but found nothing beyond a massive dose of annoyance. He glanced out the window, had a clear view of the bushy area behind the building. No sign of Mata Hari.

Too bad. If he had to wrestle with anyone, she was definitely his top choice. And it might come to that again, since he had to talk to her.

A vivid picture of her scantily clad curves flashed through his mind, bringing on a smile. She didn't seem like the type who would just roll over and give up whatever information he asked for. No matter. He had to find a way to make her talk. She was a serious threat to his cover and, as such, his life. Most importantly, she was a serious threat to his mission.

"What the hell happened in here?" Jeff, one of Mark's men, was coming in and jumped to give them a hand.

"Cyclone shook the pipes," Mark gritted out, having saved as much as he could, standing in the middle of the mess now and surveying the damage.

"Sergey should have looked." Jeff was still picking up soaked sheets of paper from the floor. "He was just up there fixing the roof."

"Let's check the other buildings—before we have more damage on our hands," Mark barked.

Jeff gave a submissive nod and took off.

Mark looked up to Cal. "I'll go drain the water so whatever is left in the pipes doesn't have to come out through here." He left without waiting for a response, used to being in charge and doing things his way.

Cal didn't mind. Even though he was the boss's cousin, he'd made no move to make himself seem important or in any way above the others since he had arrived. His goal was to blend in, to be happy-go-lucky and unassuming, gain Mark's confidence and that of the others. He was here to gather information.

And right now he wanted information on Gina Torno.

He glanced through the window again, squeezing the pipe ends together, ignoring the water that ran down his arms and into his already soaked short-sleeved shirt. What was keeping Mark?

He needed to get out of here and find that woman.

Chapter Two

"What do you mean, he caught you?" Anita's forehead tightened with tension.

Gina took a deep breath and recounted the events of the last hour, watching the path that led to their bungalow, standing in the cover of the half-open door.

"So who was he?" Sam kept an eye on the back through the bathroom window.

"What kind of computer was it?" came from Carly, who already had a gleam in her eyes. She was going through the kitchen, looking for make-shift weapons. They'd identified as many as they could upon arrival. She was now distributing them so they would be on hand if anything happened.

"You'll get your turn with the PC, I'm sure." Gina shook her head with a half smile. Carly was computer crazy. Not surprising from a former hacker.

"You bet I will." She paused midtask and

reached for a cookie on the kitchen counter under the window through which she kept an eye on the beach. "Sugarcane cookies." She made a face. "I could kill for a doughnut."

Gina winced at the word choice. Because of her, their chances of this mission ending badly just increased tenfold. How had she been stupid enough to get caught snooping around? She was surprised security wasn't already breaking down the door.

"Are you hurt?" Anita had noticed the scratch on her skin.

She shrugged it off but walked over to the kitchen to wipe off the dried blood with a wet paper towel, then returned to her post.

They were all back in the bungalow that had been provided for their use upon arrival, rustic but efficient—four bedrooms with a double bed in each and a small living room with an even smaller kitchen, plus bathroom.

The houses on the bay were all local-style, nothing fancy, not like the resort she'd expected considering that they were visiting a private island. Didn't look as though whoever owned the place spent a lot of time here.

"Did he hurt you?" Sam asked.

"We tangled a little, but I got away fine," she said.

The man did know how to move and he had a body built for fighting. "He seemed familiar." She shook her head, annoyed that she couldn't place him. "I don't know. I could barely see his face. We were both covered in dust."

Last night when they'd arrived, Mark had introduced them to a couple of people who were on the island already. But it had been dark on the beach where they'd been gathered around a tiki bar.

"Go clean up. We'll keep watch." Carly tossed her a terry towel from the back of the chair next to her, then went back to digging through the silverware drawer.

Gina rubbed the corner of the towel around her forehead and cheeks, then looked at the soiled patch. She would have liked to take a shower, but she half expected security to come for her. She didn't want to be caught at a disadvantage.

"Maybe you should get out of here," Anita said, apparently having considered the same possibility. "Find some out-of-the-way spot for a few hours until we figure out what's going on. Wish we had that map ready."

They'd begun putting together a map of the island as soon as they had arrived, starting with what was in plain view from the bay, adding to it each time they discovered a new building. They'd gone jogging on the beach that morning, then wandering around, discovering the beauty of the place. They'd familiarized themselves with the bay area, which seemed the hub of the island, starting with flatland that housed the horse stables on the east side and ending with a narrow rock cape to the west that protected it from the winds.

"There's a helipad somewhere. T keeps two choppers here," she said, sharing the newfound information with the others.

"We definitely need a location on that," Carly said.

Sam picked up a cookie. "I think Anita is right. You should go for a long walk through the woods. If they come for you—"

"And leave you to deal with it?" She shook her head. That wasn't how she worked.

"He was in the ceiling, too, whoever he is," Sam pointed out.

"Exactly." She'd been thinking about that all the way back to the others. "What was *he* doing there?"

"Could be he was trying to steal something," Sam said.

Carly fidgeted with the back of the chair. "I'd think it wouldn't be advisable to start stealing from a man like T. He's known to hold grudges."

"He has an accent," Gina remembered. "British. I think. He didn't say much."

"Do you think he's one of T's handymen?" Anita asked.

"That wasn't my impression." More intelligence shone in his blue-green eyes than all of T's goons put together. And even as he had circled her, he'd fought with elegance. His sandals had been leather, fancy brand. She closed her eyes and tried to remember the rest of his clothes. Dark shorts, pale yellow polo shirt. They were dirty. She didn't remember much else beyond that.

"Tall, well-built, midthirties, possibly British," she summed up what she knew about the man. Everyone on the island was connected to Tsernyakov one way or another. It was even possible that this guy was spying on Mark on Tsernyakov's instructions. "Even if he doesn't tell T's security about the incident, what am I supposed to do next time we run into each other?" Which was inevitable. There weren't that many people on the island, and they all lived in proximity to the bay.

"Play it by ear," Anita said. "He'll either pretend nothing happened or demand an explanation."

She'd thought about that, how she could possibly explain away why she'd been eavesdropping on Mark's meeting.

"You could say you saw some cute guy and followed him into the building to chat him up but couldn't find him. Then other people came and you got scared that you would get into trouble for going in there and so you hid," Carly suggested.

"The door to the office had been locked. I went in through the window," Gina pointed out.

Sam shrugged. "So? You were desperate."

A story like that would never fly. Gina rolled her eyes but appreciated that they were trying to help her. "If he hasn't told anyone yet and if he confronts me and threatens to, we'll have to deal with him," she said, voicing the thought that had been forming in the back of her mind for the past couple of minutes.

And she would have to be the one to "deal with him." The mission couldn't fail because of one man. They had been authorized to use deadly force from the very beginning.

"Or you turn the tables on him, track him down and demand an explanation. Do it quickly before he has the chance to talk to anyone. Determine whether he's a threat or if you can mutually blackmail each other into silence," Carly said.

She liked that idea. At least it was proactive—beat sitting here waiting for T's men to come for her. She mulled over the option.

"I don't think anyone will be coming for you," Anita said.

"How do you figure?" Sam turned to her.

"They would be here by now."

Gina looked back toward the path that led to their bungalow. Anita was right—no sign of anyone. She could see a couple of people on the beach. They all acted normal, not as if there'd been a security breach and they were hunting for the intruder.

"So he can't turn me in because he was obviously up to no good himself. I still want to figure out who he is and what he was doing up there," she said. "We need to get back out there." She nodded toward the beach and the small compound of buildings that edged it.

"We could corner him in some quiet spot," Carly said.

Gina thought for a second. "Let's hold off on the confrontation. We can always escalate later." Once they did that, there'd be no turning back. As impatient as she was for answers, for now she wanted to take the route that had the least amount of risk for breaking their cover.

"You guys should go back to mapping the place. I'll spend some time shadowing the man," she said.

TSERNYAKOV SCROLLED through his e-mails, regretting that he'd already sent Alexandra ahead to the isolated thousand-acre ranch he owned on the Peruvian highlands of the Andes. He'd been lonely last night. She had turned out to be an exceptional lover—young, nubile and eager to please. He was looking forward to being reunited with her.

In the meantime, tonight he would have some other woman brought up to his suite. He didn't see the point in self-denial, never had, but especially not now.

The end of the world as they knew it would be here in a few days. He still found it surreal to think about what was to come. From time to time he was stopped in his tracks by a wave of unease, brought on by the magnitude of the project. There was no margin for error. Zero. If he had somehow forgotten to plan for even one of the smallest details— He shoved the thought aside. He refused to consider failure. He always planned for success and he always achieved it.

He had done everything in his power to make sure he came out on top when the dust settled. He didn't relish the destruction to come, but he wasn't upset by it, either. He saw it as he saw most everything in life, good or bad—a business opportunity.

Damn politicians were always complaining about overpopulation, anyway. That problem was about to be solved. And a significant decrease in world population would bring about a significant decrease in world pollution, as well. Every cloud had a silver lining. When it didn't go against his interests, he was an environmental protectionist through and through.

He picked up his phone and sent a text message with a single word in it: *Cavanaugh.*

The response came back in a minute. *Still in the hospital. Can't talk. Prolonged recovery expected.*

Damn the man and the lifestyle he lived. Tsernyakov wouldn't have been surprised if there'd been drugs involved in the stroke. Cavanaugh worked hard, but he played hard, too.

And he wasn't easily replaced. Not at the last second.

Tsernyakov tapped the table. He hated to lose money, and it looked as if he was going to lose a lot over this. He'd barely gotten Alexeev's businesses transferred to Cavanaugh. He hated making decisions in a rush.

He picked up the phone again and sent another message, this time to Yakov. *Call me when you get to a secure location.* Now that one he'd gladly sacrifice.

SHE WAS WATCHING HIM. Under other circumstances, he would have found it flattering—she was a stunning woman. But the way things stood, Gina Torno was a serious threat to his cover. It had taken him a good hour to find her, during which several times he'd had the odd feeling that he'd been followed. He hadn't spotted anyone, however, and put the weird premonition down to the fact that getting caught by her had thrown him off axis.

She pulled a magazine from her beach bag. He rounded the tiki bar, trying to observe her without being obvious about it.

They weren't alone on the beach. A couple of his cousin's men were repairing the sand where the high waters caused by the cyclone had washed it off the beach, revealing the rocks below. Everybody seemed to be working at their leisure, not running to finish before the arrival of the boss. He wondered if that meant Joseph wasn't arriving today, either, or simply that even his staff didn't know his exact travel schedule.

Where the bloody hell was he? Cal had been waiting for a full week, albeit putting the time to good use, getting to know the island and the staff. But the kind of information he needed would come from Joseph. Cal doubted his cousin shared much about his latest project with the low-level staff on the island. And he couldn't drill Joseph until he got here.

He glanced back at Gina, half expecting to find her gone, but she was now stretched out on a beach bed. She didn't seem to be worried about him. He swallowed as she began slathering lotion on her shapely legs. She wasn't tall but perfectly proportioned, curves where they ought to be, a real woman. He recalled the smoothness of her skin when they'd fought earlier. She drew a leg up so she could smooth lotion on the back of her thigh. His loins tightened.

Was she toying with him? Trying to distract him? He needed to find out what her game was. He wanted to talk to her, figure out what she was up to and impress upon her how important it was for her to stay out of his way. He had work to do, serious reconnaissance that was better done without a witness.

He watched for another second or two before making up his mind. He would talk with her first, then head over to the doctors' accommodations since they were out spear fishing. After that he'd stop by Mark's office in the utility building and see if he could catch the guy there. He could offer to help with the cleanup and chat for a while, maybe get a clue as to why Gina had been hiding in that particular ceiling at that particular time—if she didn't tell him willingly first, for which he wouldn't hold his breath.

He glanced her way again and caught her looking. He started for her, but out of the blue the other three women appeared and took up the sun beds around her like a protective circle. Very strange. It was as if they'd been hiding in the bushes, watching. Which was ridiculous. Wasn't it?

Maybe later, then. He shook his head and

turned his back on the women, strolling toward the doctors' bungalow. Couldn't put that off any longer. He would catch Gina without her friends sooner or later. And then Ms. Torno and he would have a nice long talk. She was going to tell him what she was doing on the island, and he was going to tell her in no uncertain terms to stay out of his way.

And if she didn't, then what?

Was he prepared to make her?

The thought left a bad taste in his mouth. When he'd agreed to the mission, he'd had fighting terrorists in mind. Swarthy men with beady eyes and faces distorted by hate had been his mental image.

He wasn't scared of fighting, relished in trying himself against another in good gentlemanly fun, which his boxing club had always advocated. In addition to that, he was willing to fight for his country, for his fellow men, fight dirty if he had to, defend his own life or the lives of others.

But he felt bewildered and somewhat lost at the thought of having to fight and possibly kill a woman. Which made him realize just how big a threat to his mission Gina Torno was. Attendance on the island was by invitation only and after strenuous background checks. Her being here meant she was somehow connected to Joseph, likely a criminal just like his cousin. He couldn't afford to second-guess himself if action was required once they were face-to-face.

Another sort of action that involved Gina flashed into his mind, not for the first time since she'd come off that yacht the night before. Not going to happen. She was one of the enemy.

He reached the doctors' bungalow and knocked on the door. No response. He tried the doorknob. It twisted easily. He had brought his tools just in case, but it looked as though he would have no need for them. He pushed the door open. For a while it was time to forget about Gina Torno and focus on the task at hand.

He needed to get this done before returning to her.

"OH, MY GOD. IT'S HIM!" Sam's eyes went wide. The women were having a quick huddle on the beach, updating each other on the morning work, pretending to be tanning.

"Him who?" Gina asked as she looked after the guy she had so disastrously bumped into the day before in the ceiling. She'd been trailing him for the past hour from afar as he'd looked for her, trying to figure out what his role was on the island. She wanted to get a handle on him before she approached him. He was definitely up to something. She'd caught him following her several times the previous afternoon.

"The man in your picture," Sam said.

"Calvin Spencer? No way," Gina whispered but knew with a sudden sinking feeling that Sam was right. That's why he'd seemed so familiar. She just hadn't expected him to be here. The pictures Brant had e-mailed them had been taken in England. That night on the beach had been dark, then at the utility building his face had been camouflaged with dust and dirt from the ceiling. And today, following him, she had kept her distance.

Sam grinned. "Your future fiancé. It's fate."

That line of jokes was seriously starting to annoy her. "Let it go," Gina warned.

Brant had come through the day before they'd left Grand Cayman and gotten a name that went with the pictures. Calvin Spencer was an Englishman with a sprawling warehouse business in the U.K. He'd had one brush with the law not long ago—insider trading—but managed to beat the charges.

"So he is here," Sam said. "Why? He is a long way from home."

Anita glanced in the direction where he'd been standing. "I wonder how closely he's connected to T."

Carly raised an eyebrow at Gina. "I hope this means the wedding is off."

She pinned her with a look. "Yes. The bride will be going to the funeral of a close friend instead."

"Aw." Carly put a hand to her chest. "If that's not the sweetest threat I've ever heard. You consider me a close friend."

Gina shook her head and got up from the sun bed. "Don't make me regret it."

"Where are you going?" Anita adjusted her sunglasses—designer knockoffs, although Grand Cayman seemed to be home to an astounding number of exclusive stores that sold the real thing. Their government allowance, however, didn't allow for luxuries like that.

"Back to the utility building. I only got to check out one office. I'm pretty sure there are more. Looks like Spencer gave up on me for the morning."

"You're not going to follow him?"

"He just saw us settling in here for some sunning. If he spots me a minute later across the bay, he might figure out that I'm trailing him. I'll give him some time. I wanted to finish at the utility building anyway."

"Want us to come?" Carly asked.

She shook her head. "I can sneak around easier alone."

Anita rose, too. "Okay. If nobody needs me, I'll go back to the kitchen."

"Of course you will." Carly rolled her eyes.

Gina slipped into her flip-flops. "What's in the kitchen?"

"Pedro," Carly said with an insinuating grin. "I wonder what Brant would say to that."

"None of your business. Pedro and I are swapping recipes."

"Is that what they call it these days?"

Anita pinned Carly with an impatient look, which was very unlike her. No matter how hard they were trying to cover it up with lighthearted, smart-alecky remarks, the stress was getting to all of them. "He's been on the island for six years. He knows a lot about what's going on."

"Is he talking?" Gina perked up at the possibility.

"Not yet," Anita said. "I'm trying to establish some kind of rapport with the man." She looped her beach bag over her shoulders and took off on the path leading toward the main dining hall with long dancerlike steps. If that one couldn't get Pedro to talk, nobody could.

"I don't think Brant needs to worry," Sam said. "Notice that dreamy look on her face every time his name comes up?"

"Yeah. Love can be disgusting that way," Gina said.

"Still a skeptic?" Carly teased. "I thought you finally encountered love at first sight."

She was talking about her much regretted

remarks on Cal Spencer's picture. "And look how well that turned out," she remarked drily. "He's one of T's men."

The exasperating fact was, there *was* some initial attraction, which was more than she could say about any man she'd run into since her divorce. Go figure. The one man who'd elicited some sparks out of her battle-hardened protective armor was one of the enemy. She might as well have the hots for T himself.

Not that she had the hots for Spencer. *Absolutely not.* She could just see what the attraction might be. Not on her part. From the point of view of other women, for example the staff who seemed to smile extra wide around him and develop a sudden compulsive hip-swaying disease when he was near. She'd seen enough of that while she'd been trailing the man today.

Sam and Carly were packing up to move off. Everybody had their list of tasks to accomplish.

"Good luck," Gina said before she left them.

She took her time meandering along the path, stopping to wonder at each unusual plant, in case anyone was watching. She wouldn't have put it past Spencer to have somehow gotten behind her. She kept an eye out for him but didn't see or sense anyone at her back.

The utility building looked deserted. She stopped for a second and ran her fingers around the deep-purple flowers of a hibiscus bush while she observed the place. She didn't march straight up to the door. Instead she decided to walk around the structure first.

No repairmen this time, nobody on the roof.

She kept low and sneaked up to the window she'd gone through the day before. A man sat by the desk with his back to her. Mark? Probably. She pulled back. No sense in letting him catch her reflection in the computer screen.

She tried the next window. A jumble of wires in there but no people. The next room held wall-to-wall metal cabinets; the last room, the biggest of them all, had giant pipes running through it.

Mark seemed to be the only person in the building. She should be able to evade him. She wanted to check the rooms, make sure there were no secret passages, no hidden doors, like to an underground suite where Tsernyakov was hanging out or to some hidden lab.

This was the type of information Brant Law and the commando team on standby was expecting once the women made contact. She thought of the helipad again. Maybe they could go on a hike later and look for it. How had the doctors found it? Moseying around in the forest? Or had they been brought in on a chopper?

She made her way around the building but

didn't find a single window open. No surprise there. The air conditioner was going full blast. She circled back to the front to try the door, prepared to use her lock-picking tool kit if she had to. She'd been taking lessons from Sam.

No need for tricks, though. She found the door open.

She pushed it in carefully, peeking into the hallway. Nobody there. She slipped inside. Six doors opened from the hallway—three to the left and three to the right. She already knew that four of those opened to the rooms she'd seen from the outside. What were the other two? One could have been a bathroom, the other a storage closet. Seemed reasonable enough. Now she just had to figure out what door opened to where. Without bursting in on Mark.

She pictured the building from the outside, guessing where the rooms she'd seen were located. Mark's office would be somewhere to her right. She began her search on the left. The first room was the one with the pipes. Some kind of water-cleaning setup? There were gauges and bottles of chemicals, none of which she recognized by name. There were two small closets. She tapped the backs of both. No hidden passageways there. Gina walked to the door and listened before stepping out into the hallway.

The next door led to a small powder room, the

one after that to the room with the metal cabinets.
They were all locked, some swishing noise coming from behind them. Maybe it was all part of the
water-cleaning system along with the other room.
Once again she checked for noise from outside
before she left the room.

She'd just stepped out into the hallway when a
phone rang somewhere. She froze.

The ringing stopped.

"Dumb bastard," came Mark's voice from the
other end of the hall.

She sneaked closer.

"He better not have come back without getting it done."

She identified the room where he was talking
and stopped in front of the door to listen.

"We need the connection. That storm blew
through four days ago. Why are we still not fully
operational?" He listened for a few seconds.
"Well, dammit. If the idiot can't comprehend how
important it is, make him. He'd better get back up
there and not come down until the job is done." He
slammed down the phone.

At the same time, Gina became aware that she
was no longer alone in the hallway. She spun
around, only to see Calvin Spencer standing in
the entry door, watching her. She'd been too busy
eavesdropping to hear the outside door open.

"Lost?" he asked with his patrician eyebrow pulled up, his voice dripping with irony. "Again?"

He was definitely the guy from the picture, easier to recognize up close and without all the dust on his face. He was way better-looking than the magazine photo. His green-blue eyes held her to the spot as he walked closer.

"I was out admiring the flowers and I saw this building. Thought there might be a bathroom in here."

He tilted his head—masculine jawline, aristocratic nose, to-die-for lips—and clearly didn't believe a word she said.

She smiled to cover up how flustered she felt, then smiled wider to cover up how annoyed she was for feeling flustered. She was an ex-cop and an ex-con. Where did he get off flustering her? She'd seen her share of handsome men in her time. She was into the rugged type, anyway.

The door opened behind her.

"Hey, Cal," Mark said, then looked at her. "Can I help you?"

"Is there a bathroom in here, by any chance?" She smiled, brushing her short hair behind her ear.

Mark smiled back and pointed down the hall, and she scampered off that way. She stopped inside the door to listen.

"What's up?" Mark was asking out in the hallway.

"Came by to see if I can help."

Yeah, right. Is that what he'd been doing up in the ceiling the day before? Helping? He clearly worked for Tsernyakov. Was he stealing from the boss? Whatever he was doing, he was getting in her way at every turn. She had to get him to stop.

"The cleanup is done. Mario is bringing over some ceiling tiles later."

"So what's the damage?"

"Don't ask. It's been a hell of a day so far. Sergey just came back from the mountain."

"Satellite is back to working?" Cal asked.

"Hell, no. Stupid idiot couldn't do it."

Gina flushed the toilet to justify her being in there, silently cursing the noise that blocked out the next bit of exchange.

"Want me to take care of it?" Cal was saying outside once the rush of water stopped.

She ran the tap for a few seconds, missing some more words. Then there was no further excuse for her to stay in there, so she came out.

"Thanks. Bye." She moved past the two men, toward the door.

Cal reached for her hand and grabbed it. "Wait."

She stilled, ready to fight if she had to. She leaned in enough so a leg hook from her would send the man sprawling. Did he have a weapon? Did Mark? She measured the distance to the door.

But Cal said, "Gina wants to look at the birds on the island. I'll take her up, too."

What was he talking about? She didn't know the first thing about birds. Why did Cal Spencer want to take her up the mountain? To kill her?

Mark flashed a leering smile and clapped Cal on the back. "The tracks are washed out. There are trees across them." He glanced at Gina.

This was her chance to back out. But if she went up the mountain, she was likely to see the helipad from up there, which would be a major piece of information. The helipad would be a strategic location to be neutralized as soon as the commando team reached the island. And a trip up the mountain with Spencer would give her time to feel the man out, decide whether or not he was a serious threat to the mission, do something about it if he was.

She shrugged. "I can handle a hike." If Cal had any nefarious plans, she could handle those, too. It would be just the two of them. He could be eliminated and his death blamed on the rain forest.

Her muscles tensed at the thought. She could do it. She *would* do it if necessary. The mission was more important than any one person's life, including her own.

"Like birds that much?" Mark was grinning like a jackass.

"My favorite hobby. Go bird-watching every chance I get." *Don't ask anything about birds. Please.* What kind of tropical birds were there, anyway? Parrots were the only ones that came to mind. Seagulls? They had seagulls wherever there was water, right?

But instead of picking up the subject, Mark laughed out loud, giving her a sly look.

What was so funny?

Didn't matter. Going up the mountain with Cal would move the mission forward one way or the other. That was what counted. Another thought popped into her head that suggested she should go: from the top she might be able to get a closer look at those bunkers on the other side of the island. If Tsernyakov had something to hide, they looked like the perfect place.

Cal's hold on her loosened, but he didn't let go. "May as well leave now." The same kind of smile played on his lips as on Mark's. "Just as soon get up there before nightfall."

Up before nightfall? Her eyes went wide. How about down?

Did this mean they were going to spend the night on the mountain, the two of them, alone?

Chapter Three

Not only did she not know anything about birds, she didn't know the first thing about hiking, despite what she had told Mark. She'd been a city cop, born and raised in Philadelphia, a city girl through and through. Gina trudged behind Cal, uphill on slippery mud. Under the thick canopy, the soil hadn't yet had a chance to dry out since the last storm. They'd had to leave their four-wheelers behind halfway up the mountain.

"Watch your step," he said without turning around.

She didn't respond but kept her attention on her surroundings. Without him, she would have been lost already. She did great with city mazes, back alleys, irregular streets and winding boulevards. She knew the marks to pay attention to, could orient herself by smell alone. Chinatown had a distinct scent, as did the old industrial district and its factories that had been converted into high-priced condos, the Italian market, the park system that started behind the Art Museum, the projects.

The jungle left her feeling lost and bewildered. It seemed at the same time unknown and unknowable. The impulse to get away from here, back to something familiar, was pretty strong. The scents and noises were all different, visibility no more than twenty feet in certain spots, less when they were in an area where there was a gap in the tree canopy above and the deep-reaching sunlight nurtured a jumble of bushes and other undergrowth. She felt surrounded.

Even in the more open areas the landscape was creepy, death and destruction all around. Danger, too. The soil was still too loose; a gust of wind from the ocean could bring down more trees without notice. Then there was the danger of the man with her.

She wished she had some sort of weapon besides the steak knife she had appropriated from the kitchen. He had a nasty-looking machete hanging from his belt and a 9mm Makarov tucked into the back of his khaki pants. In plain view. Was that a warning meant for her?

She considered what it would take to get the gun away from him, and since for a moment she was focusing on the gun instead of her feet, she slipped. His hand shot out and caught her, held her steady while she found her footing.

"You dropped your torch." He bent and picked her flashlight out of the mud, then handed it to her.

"Thanks. Is that what you call it?"

He flashed a small grin that was laced with some superiority. "Proper English name."

She didn't comment. Bigger things stood between them than the language difference. "Isn't there another way up?" The mountainside was fairly steep, patches of impenetrable jungle side by side with sparser areas. There were ravines that looked dangerous and rocky slopes that seemed primed for a rock slide. They were following some sort of path that had been well used, enough so even the heavy rains couldn't wash all signs of it away.

"A few, but this is the most straightforward one. There's a path to the east that's wide enough for a truck. No good now. You can only drive it if the weather has been dry for a couple of days."

Something shrieked in the distance, the sound bringing goose bumps to her skin. "Are we safe here?"

And why hadn't she thought of that before she'd jumped into this little outing? She could have banged her head into the nearest tree, except that she didn't

want to get that close to nature. "Anything dangerous in these woods that I should know about?"

They got to a narrow, level spot and he stopped
to look at her. "Me." It was said with a smile, but
his voice had plenty of steel in it.

A clear warning. She watched him. He wasn't
a small man, his body kept in pretty good shape.
And he was up to no good, of that she was sure.
His eyes were sharp and always alert. She didn't
think he missed much. He was impressive but not
scary, the image of him tempered by his gentlemanly behavior and the British accent that she
found annoyingly sexy. She squelched that thought,
refusing to think about him in those terms.

She squared her shoulders and put on her tough-
cop face. "So what? In addition to stealing
from the boss, you also go around beating up the
guests?"

She hoped to upset his equilibrium, get him to
defend himself and slip. She needed to figure out
what he was doing on the island and she didn't
have much time. Her main priority was finding
Tsernyakov and the weapon.

One eyebrow slid up his forehead. "Stealing?
Isn't that the pot calling the kettle black?"

"I don't steal," she said with emphasis.

"Right. You sneak around and break into places
to get interior design ideas." His upper lip

twitched. He looked all cool and calm, as if enjoying himself. Hardly the picture of a man who was about to lose control and babble out information.

She didn't like him. He was too smooth by half. He thought he was humorous, did he? "What were you doing in the ceiling?" she asked in her interrogation-room voice.

He paused a beat and grew serious. "There are bigger things afoot here than you need to be involved in. Take my advice—stick to the beach and the tiki bar, have a good mini vacation, then leave."

She hated it when people patronized her. "We'll leave when we're done here." She pulled herself even straighter.

Tension crackled between them. Seconds ticked by, one after another.

He held her gaze. "One last warning. Whatever else you do, stay out of my way."

He turned before she could respond and marched forward. On their way up, he'd skirted her questions about why he'd brought her. Now it was becoming clear. To read her the riot act. If he thought—

Something dropped onto her shoulder, and she yelped when she glanced at the three-inch brown spider that was orienting itself on her shirt.

He was by her side again in a second. "Don't

move." He lifted the beast by a hind leg and tossed it into the bushes.

She did the shiver dance—hating to give such a girlie display in the middle of their power struggle but unable to help it, brushing the spot where the spider had been. *Huge* spider.

"Was that poisonous?" She rubbed her arms and shivered again. God, she hated bugs.

He shrugged. "Supposedly there are no poisonous spiders on the island. Same goes for snakes. Still, it doesn't hurt to be careful."

Exactly. Was it too late to turn around? "So what should I be looking out for? Wild boars? Mountain cats?"

"None of that. French Polynesia in general is not known for biodiversity. And this island is worse than most. Crabs, geckos, bugs, a handful of birds. That sums it up."

Now that he mentioned it, she realized that they had not, in fact, seen a single animal in the two hours since they'd started walking. *Oh.* That's why Mark had laughed at her wanting to go up the mountain for the birds. He'd probably thought— Heat flushed her face. Mark had probably thought she'd wanted to tag along so she could fool around with Cal, who was practically a stranger. And she'd said it was her favorite hobby. She winced. Great. Here for a day and building a reputation already.

Although if she ever did want to fool around with a stranger, someone like Cal would have been just fine—as long as he wasn't a criminal like this one. Walking behind him for the past two hours had given her ample time to come to appreciate his sleek but powerful figure.

"So how long have you worked for Towers?" she asked to distract herself.

"Not long."

"You manage one of his businesses?"

"I help him here and there."

"Is he on the island? I haven't seen him yet."

He shrugged.

"We're supposed to have a meeting with him."

"Then he'll probably show at some point," was the only response he gave.

"What is he like?"

"Good at what he does."

"How old is he?"

He stopped to look back at her. "Spying for the competition?"

There was that half smile of his again, but her blood ran cold from the question anyway. She still wasn't sure he hadn't brought her along to take her out. "Don't be an idiot," she scoffed.

He turned back to resume the walk. Neither of them said anything for a while.

"How come you didn't tell anyone?" She didn't

have to specify that she was talking about their incident in the ceiling. He would know.

"Who says I didn't?" he threw over his shoulder.

She stared at his back. "Did you?"

He ignored her for a while, then said, "No."

"Why?"

"Because I figured I could deal with you as effectively as my cousin's security."

"Towers is your cousin?" This was news she could take back to the team—that was good. She'd been busted by none other than Tsernyakov's cousin—that was bad. "So how do you plan on handling me?" she couldn't resist asking.

"I'll decide when I figure out who you are and what you want."

Was that a threat? Well, she wasn't scared. While he figured out how to handle her, she would figure out how to handle him. He was a threat to the mission. If she were a real spy, she would find a way to take him out here and now, just to be on the safe side. But killing a man that way went against what was inside her, regardless of what she had done in the past. She wouldn't do anything as drastic as that unless she had no other choice.

"How long are you staying on the island?" she asked.

"As long as my cousin needs me."

So much for the hope that he'd pack up and leave tomorrow.

The incline became steeper with every step they took. They walked in silence for the next hour or so, conserving energy. When they reached a rocky outcropping that had a couple of flat surfaces, he called a halt to rest.

They took off their backpacks. Hers held the food and water, his the repair kit for the satellite. Considering the number of metal tools and the spool of wire, she got the better end of the deal.

They ate canned meat, bread and fruit and each drank from their own bottle.

"I'll look around a little if you stay with the bags," he said.

"Fine." The boots he had borrowed for her rubbed her feet, anyway. She had been prepared for a beach vacation and hadn't thought to bring hiking gear.

The vegetation was lush here, so he could disappear in it in seconds. She waited a couple of minutes to make sure he was far enough. She moved over to his backpack and opened it. Tools, blanket, waterproof matches, a walkie-talkie and a fine knife with a seven-inch blade with a serrated edge. Much more effective than the kitchen utensil in her backpack. She took it and went back to her spot, leaned back on the stone to relax a little. She flipped the knife over and over again, finding its balance, getting a good feel for it.

The sun came through the leaves above, its warmth and the food she'd just eaten making her drowsy. She watched the bushes where he had disappeared, becoming mesmerized after a while by the leaves that flitted rhythmically in the breeze. Her eyelids grew heavy. She let her head rest against the rock at her back.

She slipped into the realm of dreams without notice, into the violent nightmare without any preamble. She was in a dark place. Children cried somewhere. A woman was whimpering. There was a man, the only visible shape, big and dark, made of shadows. He raged, and his fat mouth opened and there was blackness inside and something evil, threatening to swallow the crying kids, to swallow her. And he roared.

"Stop, Jimmy! Jimmy, stop!" she was yelling, knowing even in the dream that he wouldn't, aware that the end was inevitable.

A hand closed around her wrist. Hard. The pain of it brought her awake.

She had the knife in her hand and Cal holding her wrist.

"Drop it."

His face was inches from hers. She had no choice but to comply. How could she have been such an idiot and nodded off? They'd been up making plans and snooping around half the night, but still, she'd been on all-night stakeouts before and still gone to work in the morning. She was out of practice, her skills obviously rusty. A failing she couldn't afford.

He picked up the knife and tucked it away, gazed down at her from his standing position, looking pretty formidable. "Who is Jimmy?"

She was going to tell him it was none of his business, but instead she said, "A man I killed." And had the pleasure of watching his eyes go wide.

CAL LISTENED TO THE bug serenade of the night, pretending to sleep. Gina lay not a foot from him, wrapped in her sleeping bag at the base of the tower. Dusk had begun to fall by the time they'd gotten up here, thanks to the disastrous road conditions. He couldn't blame Sergey for having turned back. He would have done the same if he didn't have his private agenda.

Under the circumstances, they'd decided not to climb the tower until morning. He had plenty of time to fix what he had to and get back to the shore by midafternoon.

He opened his eyes a crack and found hers closed. The moonlight showed the curve of her hip. He tried not to focus on it much.

Gina Torno. She had killed a man. He'd been mulling that over on their way to the tower. Was she like the horde of criminals his cousin employed? Is that why she was here? He had hoped she'd come to join one of Joseph's legitimate businesses. There were plenty of those, too, to make sure the man's more nefarious activities had a solid cover.

She didn't look like the average criminals who did Joseph's dirty work. She did know how to fight, however. His still-aching ribs attested to that.

He'd brought her up the mountain so he could interrogate her away from her friends and everyone else, so he could take care of her if he decided that was the only way to save his mission. Instead he'd procrastinated the task all afternoon, asking questions but without real heat, hoping she'd betray herself on her own without him having to turn nasty.

His gut instinct and her gold-mocha eyes said she wasn't like Joseph, was nothing like Mark or the others who worked for his cousin. But there was instinct and there were facts, and the fact was that she was here at Joseph's invitation. And, in her own admission, she'd killed at least one man before.

Who was Jimmy? What had he done? The way Gina had called on him to stop in her dream, the desperation in her voice… Maybe Jimmy had needed killing. Cal watched her in the moonlight, how her face was relaxed now and peaceful—a thoroughly gorgeous woman. He would reserve judgment until he had more information on the matter.

And if she turned out to be one of the enemy and a serious risk, he would harden his heart and deal with the woman. Sometimes there was no right option; you had to make a choice between two courses of action that were bad and worse. He had known when he'd signed on to this mission that he would have to do things he'd never have done otherwise. They would have a long talk tomorrow.

Right now he had something more urgent to think about.

He sat up as quietly as he could and shook out his boots, mindful of the bugs, then slipped into them. He took nothing but his compass, gun and torch. With one last look at Gina, he slipped into the woods.

When he'd been here a week ago, he'd seen four bunkers on the south side of the island. Since he hadn't been alone, all he could do was look at them from the tower while he'd worked on the satellite dish with Sergey. The man seemed to know nothing about them, nor was he interested in discovering more.

Cal had decided then that he would come back but had had to wait until he could do so without seeming suspicious. Now was the time.

He moved with care at first, then when he figured he was out of hearing distance, he picked up speed, no longer worried if a branch snapped underfoot. He could see nothing beyond the circle of the torch. He simply followed the compass, watching where he stepped.

The jungle at night was dangerous, even if there weren't any large predators on the island. He could fall into a hole, break a leg, die before anyone found him. He just had to make sure that didn't happen. If he hurried, he could check out the bunkers and be back at the tower long before Gina woke in the morning.

A good half hour passed before he realized he was being followed.

The short hairs stood at his nape. What or who was it? Animal or human? Just because Mark said there was nothing to fear in the woods didn't mean he couldn't be wrong. Just because they'd never seen a tiger didn't mean there weren't any. There were tigers on Borneo, and that wasn't all that far away, although a much bigger island with a considerably larger habitat for big cats. He picked up speed, heading for a stand of breadfruit trees.

Whatever was following him did the same. His stalker was a human, he realized after a while and relaxed marginally, making sure his gun was handy. An animal that stalked its prey wouldn't have made this much noise.

He turned off the torch and quietly broke to the right and waited, hoping to see whoever it was pass by. Nobody came. No sound now, either. The jungle was a sheet of impenetrable darkness around him.

After five minutes or so he started out again as quietly as he could, without turning on the light. Then he tripped over a root and fell face-first into the dirt and realized as he got up how stupid he'd been. He could have been skewered by a sharp branch. He flicked on the torch again and made sure he kept it pointed at the ground at his feet, keeping it sheltered with his body from behind. Hopefully there were enough trees between him and whoever followed him to block the light.

Gina, most likely. But why? What interest did she have in his comings and goings? And if not her, then who? One of Mark's men? Had Mark somehow figured out that he had something to do with that ceiling collapse and put a man on his tail?

Cal glanced back. If he got caught snooping around those bunkers— He wouldn't. His mission was too important. He needed to make it out of the jungle alive.

He heard the noise again. Closer now, maybe only ten feet behind him. He drew his gun and turned the light off again. He had to figure out what was going on or he would never accomplish what he needed to do tonight.

He circled back to the point where he'd last heard the noise. It took him forever, but he finally saw the shadow he was looking for, standing under a nono tree in bloom. The flowers glowed in the moonlight. He moved closer inch by inch. When he was in position, he raised the torch and the gun simultaneously.

He had no time to either turn on the switch or fire. Both tools were kicked out of his hands the next second as the shadow twisted.

"Gina," he growled as they grappled with each other. He'd seen and felt enough of her height and shape to recognize her.

She was drawing back, had probably only attacked on reflex. He wouldn't let her. He had to figure out what in bloody hell was going on. He needed to grab her and not let her go until she talked.

When she was forced, she fought like a fiend, and not in a haphazard way, either. She fought like someone who'd been taught to fight. If he hadn't outweighed her, he might never have been able to get the upper hand.

As it was, he finally had her pinned against a tree, holding her hands above her head. Her chest was heaving against his. And he was glad it was dark and she couldn't see the blood that rushed to his face. From the fight, he told himself, from the exertion of the fight.

"What are you doing?"

"I wanted to see where you went."

It was somewhat gratifying that at least she was breathing hard, too.

"Who are you?"

"A business consultant."

"I already know the cover story. I want the truth. Where did you learn to fight like that?"

She waited a long time before she answered, time he spent trying to block out the sensation of her breasts pressing against him. She was full of fiery energy that in addition to putting him on guard—he knew she could go back to fighting in a split second, pulling some trick from her sleeve—was also bloody tempting.

"I used to be a cop." She bit out the words with heat, her body as tense as a drawn bow.

Disappointment flashed through him. A crooked cop, then. His cousin had a whole collection of those. "Keeping the law proved too difficult?"

So she was exactly like everyone else who worked for Joseph. What had he expected? He pulled back a couple of inches.

"You disappoint me, Gina Torno." The words slipped without his meaning to say them.

She went lax in the prison of his arms. "Welcome to the club." There was a world of regret in her voice.

Odd for one of his cousin's minions. The ones he'd met so far knew nothing of moral dilemmas or remorse.

He let her go. She shoved at him, just to prove she wasn't surrendering, he supposed, but he wasn't in the mood to play. He pinned her back up against the tree again. "I wouldn't do that one more time."

"Who the hell do you think you are to give me orders?"

"The guy who holds your life in his hands."

She laughed in his face. "You'll tell Mark about me? I wonder what he'll think about your spying on his meeting?"

"You could get lost in the woods," he said darkly. She needed to be scared enough to stay out of his way, not just in the interest of his mission but for her own sake also. If he couldn't scare her off, he would have to eliminate her. "More is going on here than you understand," he said again.

She opened her mouth, probably about to demand an explanation.

"Stay out of it and stay alive," he said.

She went completely still and seemed to consider

his words carefully, her eyebrows sliding up a quarter of an inch before she schooled her features back to normal. "Okay. Fine. You can let me go."

He did so carefully but didn't step away.

"You were going toward the bunkers," she said. "What's there?"

She was full of surprises, this one. "How do you know about the bunkers?" How closely was she involved in Joseph's despicable projects?

"Our ship came around that corner of the island."

"How many?"

"Four."

That's how many he'd seen from the tower. He'd wondered if there were more, blocked by vegetation or one of the large boulders that dotted the hillside that way.

"What are they?" she asked.

"Military bunkers left over from World War II." He wasn't giving away anything by telling her that. He knew little more himself.

"Why are they important to you?"

"They aren't."

"That's why you were risking your life in the dark sneaking over to them in the middle of the night?"

She sure interrogated like a cop.

"What's it to you?"

"I want to go with you." She tilted her head. "Why?"

"I'm scared to stay alone in the woods."

Right. She might have been good at cop stuff, but she wasn't good at lying. Odd for a criminal.

Myriad unlikely thoughts zipped through his head, possibilities he hadn't considered before.

What if she wasn't just like the others his cousin employed? What if she was here for the same reason he was, sent in by the Americans?

The thought stopped him in midmotion.

But wouldn't the SIS, Britain's Secret Intelligence Service, who had recruited him for this job, have told him if there were other operatives in the field? And what if SIS didn't know about the Americans?

They had to, didn't they? They were allies. These sorts of things were coordinated.

He collected his torch first, then, with its help, his gun.

"You're going to shoot me?" Her body language was relaxed, but from the sharp look in her eyes he knew she was poised to fight.

"I probably should." She knew enough to cause serious trouble. But she hadn't yet. And she seemed to be doing the same type of information gathering on the island as he was, the reason they were continuously getting in each other's way. Was he right about her being undercover? Could they work together? Did he have a choice?

What if she was here from some U.S. agency, they didn't share information and ended up blowing the mission for nothing but stupid mistrust? He had to take a chance on her. If she wasn't who he thought she might be… He rubbed the back of his hand over his forehead. He would deal with that if and when he came to it.

"Now what?" she asked.

He couldn't believe he was seriously considering leveling with her. His contact at SIS would have a fit. But his contact wasn't here to assess the situation and make decisions.

"Who are you working for?" He trained the light on her face.

She squinted. "Savall. You know that. It's just a consulting company," she said with bravado, but he could read the truth behind her words. He was a seasoned businessman who'd been through his fair share of negotiations. He knew when someone was stonewalling him.

He raised his gun. "You got yourself into something really nasty. I'm sorry. I'm going to ask one *last* time. It's vital that you give the right answer, Gina. Who are you working for?"

Time and tension stretched between them as she measured him up, staring at him wildly. He could see the wheels madly turn in her head. Then she came to some sort of decision and squared her shoulders, bracing herself for whatever was to come.

He didn't miss the hand that sneaked behind her back. She probably had some sort of weapon. How? From where? Joseph's men wouldn't let anyone bring weapons to the island. He'd had to ask Mark for his gun and knife with the excuse that he wished to explore the jungle. He knew he was fully expected to give back both upon his return.

She drew in a slow breath and held it. "I'm working for the U.S. government." She seemed ready to spring.

"For whom?"

"Who are *you* working for?" she asked instead of answering.

He hesitated. Didn't really have any other choice but to tell her, did he? They needed to form some sort of an alliance.

"SIS." He watched for her reaction.

Surprise and relief. "British Intelligence? They got you to go after your own cousin?"

His mood slipped and his defenses rose. He was well aware that he was going against family, had refused the mission over and over until SIS provided him with unquestionable proof that his cousin was a criminal mastermind who was responsible for the deaths of tens of thousands and was now part of a terrorist plot that could endanger millions.

He put that thought aside, aware that even though he'd taken on the task, his feelings were far from resolved.

"We're on the same side," he said, emphasizing the most important thing.

"Prove it. Give me one of your weapons."

"Show me yours."

She waited a beat, then pulled a steak knife from behind her back. And he could tell from her eyes that she would have gone up against him without a second thought. She had plenty of pluck.

He considered her for a moment and handed over the machete, a deadly weapon in its own right. She put away the knife and ran her fingers over the long blade, took a few seconds to examine the weapon. On their way up the hill, he'd kept it from her when she'd asked for it to help clear the underbrush.

"Not bad," she said and swung it with purpose to try her hand, giving him second thoughts about having handed the blade over.

"What would you have done if I turned out to be Towers's man through and through?" he asked out of curiosity.

She didn't even blink. "You would have had an unfortunate accident in the woods."

Chapter Four

"So how long have you known Towers?" Gina asked as they moved forward in the night. The going was easier now that they were walking downhill, but they still had to watch their footing to make sure they didn't slide on the soggy soil.

She was relieved to be walking with Cal. Following him through the night jungle had been a nerve-racking experience. She'd been scared stiff thinking she might lose sight of him and get lost.

"Most of my life, I suppose, in the sense that I knew of him. You know, the family grapevine. As far as the aunts and uncles know, he's a successful businessman, all legit. We didn't meet until a couple of months ago." He sounded uneasy.

"So how did you two end up meeting?"

He hesitated.

"We're on the same side," she reminded him.

He walked on, watching the narrow forest path

they were following. "I'm glad, actually." He glanced over. "It's a good feeling not to be alone in this." He flashed that half grin of his. "I'm sure that's not terribly macho to admit."

"I'm glad we're coconspirators, too. The others will feel the same." She hoped. She'd already told Cal about Carly, Sam and Anita. He'd guessed most of it anyway, since they'd come to the island as a team, together. "So how did you hook up with Towers?"

"The Secret Intelligence Service set him up," he said after a while. "I was approached by the SIS. They somehow figured out that I was a distant relation. They tracked me down, told me about what he was doing in the world and asked if I would cooperate." His voice sounded a little off.

"Torn loyalties?" she guessed.

"He's a bloody bastard, no question. But at the end of the day…he's still family, you know?"

She nodded. Her family was back in Philadelphia, thinking that she was in some kind of an experimental program somewhere in the U.S. that was readying her for reentry into society. They didn't care that she'd done something that was colossally stupid, not to mention a capital crime. They kept right on loving her without pause. Tsernyakov, alias Joseph Towers, was on a whole other scale, however. She told Cal that much.

"How about your family?" he asked after a while.

"They know nothing about this, that's for sure." She didn't feel like giving him the details of her meltdown as an officer of the law and her subsequent conviction and the deal she'd eventually made with the government. It was enough for him to know that she worked on the right side.

"Husband and kids?"

She shook her head. "Seven sisters. Traditional Italian family. Pop kept trying for a boy. Wife and kids waiting for you at home?"

"Hold on, I'm still stuck on the seven sisters thing. Stunning concept. I'm an only child." He shook his head. "Frankly I find the idea of eight rambunctious girls running around in the same house a tad frightening."

"Rambunctious—yes. Girls—not so much. My youngest sister is twenty."

He flashed a smile that was the devil's own. "So we are talking about eight beautiful women. They must look at least a little like you." He let his gaze sweep over her. "I'm warming up to the idea."

He thought she was beautiful? She felt flustered and covered it by going on the offensive. "What does your wife think about you taking off to the other side of the world on an undercover mission?"

"No wife," he said with a look that seemed to

insinuate that he knew she'd been fishing for that piece of information with a purpose.

She was so *not*. She glared at him.

"But don't get your hopes up. Confirmed bachelor." He flashed a cocky grin.

She put her nose in the air. "As if."

"Are you close to your family?"

"They are… We're close." And she would be back in the thick of things again once she went home. But what would she do once she returned? She could never go back to her old job….

The path. The bunkers. The mission.

That was the only thing that mattered right now. If their mission failed, she would never see her family again. A fact that Cal had to be aware of, as well. "How about your parents?"

"We're close, even the greater family," he said, plodding after her. "Even with the Russian branch. My mother keeps in touch."

"So what did Towers want from you? Is that his real name?" He seemed to want to avoid the subject. Too bad. She was good at keeping focused.

"Joseph Tsernyakov," he said. "He told me he changed it to Towers a few years ago because he had some global businesses coming in and Westerners felt more comfortable doing business with a familiar name."

She felt a weight lift from her. So Towers *was*

Tsernyakov. This was the first real confirmation they had. They got to him. God, it had seemed impossible at the beginning, but somehow they had managed. She grinned into the semidarkness, feeling light-hearted all of a sudden. But not so much as to forget the question she was seeking an answer to.

"So what are you doing with him here?"

He took a deep breath. "This is all classified information."

The wind was picking up, shaking the canopy above.

"I think we've moved beyond that."

He thought for a while.

"SIS recruited you...." she prompted him.

"Right. They set up a scenario where I got in trouble with the law. Insider trading. A big fuss was kicked up over it. I lost some business." That last sentence was said in a tight voice. "The family was mobilized, of course. Then, the next thing I knew, Joseph was stepping up to the plate, clearing the way for a dismissal of charges."

That was what family was for when you were in trouble. Hers stood by her to the end, showing up in court every single day, supporting her every way they could. She was doing this for them.

"He needed access to my warehouses in England," he said somberly.

Given the business Tsernyakov dealt in—illegal

weapons trade—she had a few ideas about what he meant to store. "Was that why you were in the business papers? Because of your indictment?"

"It had to look like it was all for real. Got a lot of publicity. I've been working my way up to the top in the U.K. and just signed some major contracts with China."

He was probably losing a good chunk of business and a ton of money over this. He had put his reputation and livelihood, not to mention his life, on the line for this mission. The choice had been an easy one for Gina. She had nothing to lose. Cal stood to lose everything. She squelched the grudging sense of admiration that bubbled up from some unexamined corner of her mind. She'd decided to trust him because it was in the best interest of her mission. She drew the line at liking the man. He was too full of himself by half already.

"So what does SIS have on him?" she asked.

The wind was now howling on the bay side of the island. The treetops shook above them, but the mountain was blocking the worst of the weather.

"They think he hired a handful of rogue scientists to make a modified version of the smallpox virus that's vaccine-resistant."

She gasped, her mind lurching into overdrive as she considered the implications. This was major new information for her team. A huge piece of the puzzle.

"The FBI and the CIA didn't know that?" He cut into her thoughts.

"All we have is a date. November twenty-seventh." She didn't want him to think she was coming to their alliance empty-handed.

His turn to be surprised, it seemed, because he stopped in his tracks, his eyes going wide. "That's five days from now."

The thought sobered them both.

"Bloody murder. Sure wish the people we work for coordinated with each other."

So did she. And there was no way to get that information back to Brant and Nick now. They had no way to communicate with anyone off the island, although Carly was diligently working on combining their four cell phones and the radio in their bungalow into some sort of a super communication device. She was a whiz with everything that ran on a chip and could be programmed. If anyone could do it, she'd be the one. "Maybe they were each extra cautious considering T's extensive grid of paid men in every branch of law enforcement in most every country that counts." She listened to the wind. "You think another cyclone is coming?"

"Just some strong winds. I've been tracking the weather-service announcements. There's a new cyclone forming to the east of us, but it's way out at sea. We're not in the projected path this time."

Cal rubbed his hand over his forehead. "So what's the date? Handover of the virus to the terrorists or the day of the attack?"

She shrugged. "We don't know. Could be one and the same."

"Good God."

He said that with such English tone and expression, if their situation wasn't so dire, she would have smiled.

They reached a semiopen area. Dawn was breaking somewhere over the ocean, the sky lightening. They'd walked and fought through most of the night.

"We have to be close," he said.

She glanced up the tree they were passing under and paused. "I'll go up and look around."

"Sounds like a plan." He gave her a hand.

And since having him touch her felt more than a little disconcerting, she shimmied up the tree extra fast—not an easy task as, even with the mountain blocking most of the wind, the branches swayed precariously.

"Anything?" he yelled up when she was a good thirty feet off the ground.

"Vertigo," she joked.

"I'll catch you if you drop."

The funny thing was, even though they were just kidding around, she knew he would. He was competent, had stepped up to the plate each and every time so far.

"I think I see something." She squinted toward the east. "About a half a mile from here."

"Very well. We should get going," he said and watched as she climbed back down.

They cut through the jungle without trouble, more and more light available from above, and reached the structure at full daybreak, approached it carefully to make sure they didn't run into Tsernyakov's guards. The bunker appeared deserted.

A fifteen-minute observation confirmed that first impression. Gina kept an eye on Cal as they circled the place. He moved well for a guy who had supposedly only gotten a month of training from SIS.

The low entry door, no more than four and a half feet tall and covered in rust, was a formidable steel monster, sealing the square cement structure. Locked, of course. She stared at the old-fashioned lock and wished Sam were there. Sam could open just about anything.

"Mind if I give it a go?" he asked, fiddling with his flashlight.

"Go ahead."

He neatly twisted off the back where the batteries were stored and pulled out several long metal picks.

"Nice."

He gave her a wicked smile. "I try to be prepared."

For the next couple of minutes he worked the lock without success, however. "Didn't say I was an expert." But just as he said the last word, the door did pop open.

She looked to the inside frame immediately to check for sensors and signs of an alarm system. There didn't seem to be any. The reason became obvious once they aimed their flashlights farther in: a second door blocked the narrow area about five feet from the first.

They ducked their heads and stepped in.

"Seems more sophisticated." She looked at the stainless-steel second door and the LCD-display keypad on it.

"Would you like to give it a try?" he asked, all gentlemanly manners.

"You got any more secret tools?"

"I might have a little something," he said modestly and took his watch off and popped the back cover.

He pulled two thin wires and attached them to the keypad while she did her best to keep her chin from dropping.

"SIS has a lot of gadgets." And, of course, as a trusted family member, Cal had greater freedom sneaking his tools onto the island. Her team hadn't dared bring anything.

"I think it's the whole *double-oh-seven* pressure. They must try to live up to the myth."

"My team has a lock expert, too—Sam," she said to let him know they hadn't come completely unprepared.

He was too focused on what he was doing to respond.

Once again it took a couple of tries, but he got the door open after a few minutes. She checked for a security system. Nothing here, either. Maybe Tsernyakov thought the bunkers were impregnable. Or he wanted as few people involved in their secret as possible and didn't want to risk a security team coming in to wire up the place. The two doors could have been made someplace else, then put in here by a simple mason. One man who could easily be made to disappear.

Was she getting too paranoid about Tsernyakov? She didn't have time to ponder. Cal was already searching the twenty-by-twenty-foot room, poking at the floor-to-ceiling pile of cardboard boxes inside.

"What is it?"

He opened one of the boxes. "Five-gallon jugs of mineral water."

She moved to the other side of the narrow aisle among the boxes and pulled one out enough so she could jiggle the sealing tape aside and take a peek inside with the help of her flashlight. "You won't believe what this is."

"MREs?" He came over.

Meals Ready-to-Eat. Dehydrated food packages manufactured for and used by the U.S. armed forces. "How did you know?"

"Joseph rented a couple of my warehouses in the north of England. Same stuff there."

"He is laying in supplies."

He nodded, scanning the towering mass of boxes, halting the circle of light on a wood door in the back.

"Allow me," she said, feeling as though she hadn't contributed much to their alliance so far, eager to demonstrate that she could handle what came her way.

She balanced on her left leg while pulling the right up and in, giving a formidable kick to the door. It flew open with a crash. She bit back a smile of satisfaction.

"It wasn't locked." He bowed slightly and gestured her forward with a hand.

What? She looked at the door frame as she stepped in. Damn. She glanced back at him. If he gave the slightest sign of mocking her, she would wipe the smirk off his face. But he seemed focused on the task ahead already, panning the room that was much smaller than the main area of the bunker. More boxes occupied the space here, each stamped with *Rx*.

"Drugs?" she asked.

He opened a box and held it up for her. She caught a name on one of the shrink-wrapped packages inside, well-known antibiotics.

When she looked up, the usual carefree smile was gone from Cal's face. "How long is he planning on hiding out? How much damage is this virus expected to make?"

"What does SIS think?"

He shrugged, frustration sitting on his face. "I know the setup and what I need to do, not much beyond that."

"I doubt this is all for him and the few he plans to save to serve him. This is probably stock he wants to sell at ten times the price once all hell breaks loose."

He looked around, seeming to consider her words, then nodded.

"What's that?" A low tunnel behind a stack of boxes had caught her gaze. It seemed to be carved into the hillside, not much more than a crawl space.

"My guess would be an emergency exit." He was striding over and sticking his flashlight and upper body inside already.

"Should we go in and see where it leads?" She walked up behind him.

"Not far. The tunnel has collapsed." He stepped aside so she could see.

Rocks blocked the way, looking as if the collapse had happened some years ago. "So we're done here?"

"Wish we knew more." He shook his head as if he were shaking off his frustrations. "We should make haste. We have three more buildings to check and the satellite to fix, plus getting back to the beach before nightfall. If we stay too long, somebody might find it suspicious."

They put the boxes they'd moved back into place and locked the doors behind them.

She looked back at the bunker as they were walking away. Another clue. And still not enough. They were racing to discover more, always coming in short of the goal. And they were running out of time.

SHE WAS GORGEOUS AND tough and very capable. If he had to be trekking through the jungle with anyone, his first choice was definitely Gina Torno. Cal moved forward among the breadfruit trees.

"What's that?" Gina was pointing to a small fruit-laden evergreen tree a little ahead.

"Nono fruit. Supposed to be very healthy." The

trees flowered and produced fruit year-round. "According to Mark, it's becoming a major business on some of the other islands."

He was becoming familiar with the island's limited flora, had used it as an excuse to wander around and discover the place in the first few days. Coconut palms lined the beaches, guava and taro growing in great abundance on the south side of the island. "Hungry?"

She nodded, so he veered off the path and she followed and picked a handful of yellow fruit.

"Hold on. It's ripe when it's white and the skin is thin. Don't expect much." He'd tried the plum-size fruit before and found it unpleasantly bitter.

She took the white, ripe one he offered and made a face when it neared her nose. "Not too appetizing."

"Smells sort of rancid, doesn't it?"

She nodded, wiped the fruit on her shirt and bit off a chunk. "It has seeds."

"Lots of them."

She finished it with a less-than-enthusiastic look on her face. A drop of juice ran down her chin. She wiped it off, then licked her lips to remove the last of it. He didn't think she'd meant the gesture to be tempting; she wasn't even looking at him but was staring at the tree, considering. His mouth went dry all the same.

She had great lips, full and ruby-red, glistening

with juice at the moment. Lips like that should be required to carry a license.

"I don't see how this can be big business." She wrinkled her nose. "I can't see it catching on."

He reined in his wayward thoughts and focused on her words. "It has already. It's the latest all-natural miracle dietary supplement, if you believe the ads."

She reached for the nearest branch. "Worth a try, isn't it? I've been so—" she hesitated "—tied up in the last couple of years I haven't had a chance to try many new things or keep up with what's going on."

He could only imagine. Being a cop wasn't a relaxed, nine-to-five type of position.

They filled up whatever empty space they could find in their backpacks before moving on.

"Forgot. I've got a bag of peanuts, as well. Would you like some?" He reached into the side pocket of his backpack and dragged the bag out.

She accepted a handful, and they snacked on those for a while.

"Last nut." He emptied the bag into her hand, then crushed the empty bag into his pocket as he turned to the path.

"Hardly," she said to his back.

He grinned but didn't turn.

The next bunker was half a mile in the direction of the beach. It turned out to be pretty much the same as the first. Same security, same content.

The escape tunnel was walled off with cement bricks and mortar.

Another twenty-minute hike took them to the third bunker, another gray, square building, a little higher up the hillside. It turned out to be just like the first two, inside and out. He was beginning to give up hope that they would find anything relevant.

The sun was high in the sky by the time they reached the smallest bunker, the most difficult of the four to get near as it was built on a dangerously steep incline. They practically had to pull and push each other up, and that got him splendidly close to Gina and her many charms. Which reminded him that, although he was acting out a serious boyhood fantasy playing the role of some super-spy, he was first and foremost a man, and his manly fantasies looked a lot like the woman dangling from a protruding tree root above him.

Normally when he'd been this close to a woman and they had touched each other this much, he expected some sort of satisfaction at the end for the both of them. Gina Torno, however, was nothing but a source of frustration. As far as he could tell, she wasn't even aware of him as a man.

He was a confirmed bachelor, not a confirmed monk. What was wrong with her, dammit?

She slipped a good foot, bringing her temptingly round behind inches from his face. He bit back a groan.

"Allow me to help." He grabbed her boots and gave her some leverage, pushed her up by her feet.

She rolled onto the slight plateau by the bunker's opening, extended her arm down to him and helped him up.

"Can't see much being up here." Her breathing was a bit more labored than usual, her face flushed, her eyes shining from the exertion.

For a second he forgot all about the bunker and just stared at her as she lay on her back, trying to catch her breath. Maybe he looked too long.

"Hurt yourself?" she asked with some concern.

"No. Fine." He stood before he made a bloody fool of himself, hoping she hadn't seen the naked desire in his eyes.

What was wrong with him? He should be one hundred percent focused on the mission. He'd never had any trouble separating fun from business before. He turned his back on Gina with purpose and focused his attention on the bunker.

The door was just as old and rusty as the ones before, sporting the same sort of lock. He got his tool kit out and got started. It went easier this time; he'd had practice with the other three. Since this bunker was smaller than the rest, the ante-chamber was tighter, which he'd pretty much expected, a space no more than six or seven square feet. The secondary door, however, did provide a surprise.

"What's this?" Gina asked.

"Reinforced steel. And a lovely security up-grade." He stared at the entry keypad. "Something special is in there, isn't it? Question is, do we want to know what?"

He didn't have to spell it out. The virus could be behind the door.

"Best-case scenario." She looked nervous but nodded.

"It'd be brilliant, wouldn't it?" If the virus hadn't been handed over to the terrorists yet and if they had the exact location of it, there was a good chance for stopping the whole disaster.

"I was given the antiserum for smallpox a few weeks ago." Though the new strain was supposed to be vaccine-resistant, so that could provide little or no protection. Still. "I'll go first. You stay here and wait until I figure out what's inside."

"*If* we can get in." She nodded toward the keypad.

"There's that. You think Samantha could do it?" Maybe they could sneak her up here somehow, get her away from the bay with a clever excuse.

GINA WATCHED AS HE took stock of the lock, examining it from every angle. Could Sam do better?

"I don't know. She's had some experience with locks but not fancy ones like this. But then she got extra training." She shrugged, wishing that the rest of her team were here.

Sam had been a child of the streets in her teenage years and had gotten into plenty of trouble with the law. But she had done petty-crime stuff mostly, stealing food to stay alive. Maybe it was wrong, but even as an ex-cop Gina had trouble judging her for that. Now Sam was a valued member of the team. It was thrilling, actually, to watch the woman she was becoming. They had changed in the past few months, all four of them.

He was hooking up his watch to the keypad and pushing the tiny buttons on the side of the timepiece. Numbers scrolled down the LCD display. One minute passed, then another.

"How long is it going to take?" She looked outside at the sun that was high in the sky.

"No idea."

Not too encouraging.

"So if you need to get in touch with your people, how do you do it? Sneak a call from one of Tsernyakov's phones?"

He shook his head without taking his eyes off his work. "I go fishing."

She waited for explanation and when none was

forthcoming she said, "Oh, the phone fish. Of course. Used them in the past. Hard to catch."

He looked over at her and grinned before returning his attention to the watch again. "The nearest island, Hariumat, is only about fifty nautical miles from here. I go into harbor and stop for lunch at a local restaurant. My connection keeps a secure mobile phone hidden for me in the restroom."

She wondered if Brant's commando team, which was supposed to be on standby, was waiting for contact on the same island. Their mysterious host had not revealed the exact location when he'd invited them, but the yacht they'd boarded had been followed via satellite. That way the commando team charged with seizing Tsernyakov and the weapon would know where they were and could take up positions nearby, waiting for communications from the four-woman team.

Waiting in vain, since communications from the island were strictly controlled.

"You think when we get back from fixing the satellite you could take me fishing?"

The watch beeped. He stopped fiddling with the buttons and turned toward her with a cocky smile. "Another date so soon? It's becoming a serious relationship, isn't it? Well, Americans do move fast. I've been warned."

"In your dreams, Spencer."

But he wiggled his eyebrows suggestively as he pushed the door open.

Her smile faded. "We're in." Her voice was on the squeaky side.

He nodded, growing somber, too. "You wait here."

She moved into position so she could at least see inside. A tunnel started just behind the door; she could see nothing beyond the first bend.

"I was hoping we might find some biohazard suits. Would make me feel more comfortable." Not to mention being a clear sign that they were in the right place. "Take my camera," she said.

He drew up an eyebrow as she took off her ring. "Aim the gemstone, then push here."

"Brilliant." He nodded and jammed it onto his pinkie finger. It only went up to the second knuckle.

"Be careful," she called after him.

"Don't worry. I wouldn't miss our next date for anything," he said with a slow grin just before he disappeared around the bend.

THE TUNNEL SYSTEM was a bloody maze, side corridors leading off now and then abruptly. He investigated each, only to end up staring at a land collapse or a walled-off dead end after having wasted precious minutes. His compass came in handy. It wasn't the sort of place anyone would enjoy being lost in.

Cal strode forward, taken by surprise when a glint of light caught his eye. A moment passed before he realized it was his own torch reflected in the stainless steel door that closed off the way. It had a simple key lock. Whoever had thought up security probably figured nobody would get this far.

He popped the lock and looked around a conspicuously empty room. Were they too late? Was this where the virus had been? Had the handover happened already?

A round steel door with odd spokes at the back of the room, the kind you'd see in bank robbery movies in the walk-in safes, caught his attention. He stared at it for a moment and blinked. His watch wasn't going to do much with that.

He walked up to it anyway and took a number of pictures. Might come in handy yet. They needed to ask for outside help with this one. Did his cousin keep his emergency cash here?

A soft buzzing filtered through from inside the safe. He stilled. What was that? It seemed like some kind of machinery. A generator? For what?

Refrigeration. The answer popped into his mind and sped his heart rate.

If he was right, it could mean only one thing:

the virus was on the island and at this moment within arm's reach.

They had to get the commando team here before that changed.

Chapter Five

"Yes, sir," his secretary said. "I will notify them right away."

Tsernyakov didn't like the look in the man's eyes.

"I will change the date of our meeting as many times as I feel necessary until I'm sure that there is no way our security has been compromised." Not that he owed his secretary an explanation, nor the School Board—the terrorist organization that was his buyer for the virus. They'd probably been giving his secretary hell over the frequent changes in parameters in the last week or so.

He was getting antsy, feeling on the edge. It had been a long while since he'd worried about anything like this. Not that it wasn't understandable. Never before had he had this much at stake.

"Certainly, sir. Anything else, sir?"

He shook his head and waited until the door

closed behind the man before phoning Mark on the island.

"Everything okay?" He listened to the status report on the postcyclone repairs. There were a million things going on and he had to keep on top of it all. "How about the satellite?"

"Cal is fixing it as we speak."

His cousin had turned out to be a useful man all around. He preferred to keep his family out of his business, but in this case it looked as if he had made the right decision. Cal was smart, a quick learner and not overly scrupulous. "The guests are enjoying themselves so far?"

"I don't think the doctors want the positions." Mark sounded apologetic.

As he should. It was his job to take care of that piece of the project.

"I'll talk to them when I get there. I still don't know when I can get away from here." He kept his comings and goings a secret even from his most trusted men—the reason he had been able to avoid a number of assassination attempts and police raids in the past. "How about the women from Savall?" He had plenty of work for them once he got to the island. He needed to move money around and he wanted to be able to keep a close eye on the transactions. Their luck. As long as they pleased him they would be saved.

"They ask about you."

A certain amount of curiosity was only natural. "I'll be there soon."

He looked around his office as he hung up. The space was close to bare. The hum of an industrial-size shredder came from beyond the door. His secretary and a couple of clerks were making sure everything was cleaned up. He would leave no incriminating evidence behind. He wanted to personally make sure of that before he left.

His sixth sense was prickling. Had he forgotten something? Was his subconscious picking up on an odd clue or odd behavior from someone around him? He thought over the events of the week so far, but nothing jumped out. Maybe he was simply getting tired from all the rush that was leading up to the big day.

Too many details required his personal attention on this job. He was running himself ragged and he didn't like the feeling but was unwilling to delegate more, unwilling to trust others who could betray him later. All the crucial aspects of the job he held in his own hands, the only way to be sure.

He thought of Alexandra. It wouldn't be much longer now. Soon he would get his much-deserved break.

IT HAD TAKEN THEM several hours to make it from the bunkers to the satellite tower, part of which time

Cal had spent by telling her about his discovery in the last bunker. Her mind kept returning to that. Was it really possible that they'd found the virus?

"No. That one." Cal pointed, hanging on to the metal structure with one hand. The height didn't seem to bother him.

Gina, on the other hand, hated to let go of her handhold but did it anyway to pass him the tool he was asking for. She didn't mind the dangling; she hated the dizzying distance that separated her from the ground.

When she had both hands firmly on the metal bars again, she glanced toward the helipad one more time and the two choppers that sat on the ground about halfway between the tower and the bay, toward the east side of the island. The place seemed abandoned from up here. She could see the road that Cal had talked about, the one that could handle a pickup truck. It wound its way not far from the path that came up to the tower, ending at the helipad. They probably used it to transport the supplies they flew in. All good, important information she needed to pass on to Brant Law as soon as she managed to make a connection.

"So tomorrow morning we go out fishing, then you take me to lunch. We'll both call in the information we have and try talking our respective connections into working with each other," she said, rehashing their plan, thinking it over one more time to make sure they hadn't missed anything.

"And hope they will."

Their goal seemed so close. They were in the hold-your-breath-and-hope-nothing-else-happens stage of the operation. "Why wouldn't they?"

He tightened the screw. "Tsernyakov is a pretty big trophy."

Cal thought rivalry was going to be a problem? "There's too much at stake for them to mess this up over who gets credit."

"I hope." He kept his attention on what he was doing, talking without looking at her. "Copper wire."

"How do you know all this?" He really was pretty impressive in a number of ways, a self-reliant kind of guy, which she appreciated.

"I was up here with Sergey last week. Same problem. I watched him fix it. They need a new setup, but until it comes in they have to keep patching this one."

"You seem to be good at this kind of stuff."

"I like tinkering."

She took the screwdriver from him and put it away in the tool case. Dropping something was to be avoided at all costs. They'd have to climb all the way down to retrieve it, then back up. *If* they could find it in the thick vegetation around the tower's feet. Since trees had been cut around the structure, enough sunshine reached down to support a host of shrubs and climbers.

"My father did, too." He had been always working on something, fixing various appliances for people on their block in his free time.

"Was your father a cop?"

"My mother," she said, and he glanced at her with surprise in his eyes.

Granted, being a police officer wasn't a common occupation for a traditional Italian-American housewife, especially in her mother's generation. But her mother wasn't exactly an average woman. She could break up a pub fight, put away a score of drunkards, then come home and whip up lasagna like it was nobody's business, help her girls with their homework and clean house before she went to bed. Of course, the older girls helped out a lot, too. "My father was a fireman."

"My father was in the jewelry business. Mum stayed home. She was on a lot of committees— Immigrant Assistance League and all that. She's retired now for the most. Hold here."

She gripped the steel support he was trying to push into place. She didn't know any jewelers; people like that didn't live in her neighborhood. She watched Cal and that smooth air he possessed. They'd sure come from different backgrounds.

And yet she felt pretty comfortable around him. He seemed like a down-to-earth, easygoing guy now that he wasn't trying to intimidate her. "Done?"

"Almost."

She angled her wrist so she could see her watch. Five o'clock. They needed to hurry so they could get back to the beach before dark. She wondered if the girls had been able to turn up anything new while she'd been gone. She was eager to tell them of her discoveries. As much as they'd protested her going up the mountain with Cal, they were going to like the results.

"View's brilliant from up here, isn't it?" He smiled at her as he lowered himself to the same level where she was.

She bit back a groan. She hadn't dared to look more than was absolutely necessary. She'd been keeping her attention strictly on the tower, on her next step, on what they were doing, on Cal and the easy conversation between them, with occasional peeks at the helipad. They were on top of a tower on top of a mountain. "Given the choice, I wouldn't come up here for sightseeing."

He came over to her and put his arms around her from behind, turning her toward the east. Now he made her nervous. She tried not to look as awkward as she felt. But after a few moments she got used to his nearness and leaned against the support of his body. And for the first time she felt safe enough to really look out over the rain forest that spread at their feet.

Breathtaking.

Blooming trees dotted the forest, disrupting the green canopy with color. There might not have been a huge diversity of birds on the island, but the beauties they did have sunned themselves on the treetops, harvesting insects and fruits. The sand seemed pink from a distance, the ocean a mesmerizing azure. She took a slow breath and filled her lungs with the exceptional beauty of the place, forgetting for a moment her precarious perch and even the mission.

"So?"

"Beautiful." The word didn't do it justice. She was glad that she had come up the mountain with him, even beyond the information she'd been able to gain.

He turned her in the circle of his arms. Since she was clinging to him with one arm now, their faces were only inches apart.

His blue-green eyes matched the ocean, the color seeming to swirl as the waves were doing in the distance. Awareness blossomed between them, taking her by surprise, making her wonder if he felt it, too. Cal Spencer. He was not at all the type of man she was normally attracted to. So why was she at this moment wishing that he'd keep holding on to her?

His gaze dropped to her lips.

Her heart just about stopped.

He wasn't thinking what she thought what he was thinking, was he?

"If I don't kiss you now, I'll never forgive myself," he said with a half smile.

She was too stunned to protest.

The next second his warm mouth was on hers. Not crushing and wild with passion but not tentative, either—a firm, tantalizing kiss from a man who seemed to know exactly what he wanted and wasn't afraid to go for it.

She wasn't sure whether it was the height or the kiss that made her dizzy, but she found herself tightening her grip on him.

He took his time, still smiling when he pulled away. "I quite fancy you, you know."

She blinked. "Are all Britons this straight to the point?"

His only response was a widening grin.

She tried to pull away from him a little. She needed distance to process what had just happened.

"Right." He let her go. "I'd love nothing more than to stay up here snogging with you the rest of the day, but I suppose we better make our way to the ground and get back before Mark sends out a search team. I'll go first," he said. "To catch you if you fall."

She did have a sense of falling just then and it had nothing to do with the tower. No, no, no. She wasn't going to go there. The kiss—*snogging,* as he'd put it—had been nothing but an impulsive act brought on by the beauty of the moment and their stunning surroundings.

She was not going to obsess over it, was not going to make herself look ridiculous by demanding an explanation. She was going to forget it and put on an air of cool European elegance about the whole thing, to which he was no doubt accustomed.

She just needed to figure out how to go about it.

KISSING HER MIGHT NOT have been the smartest thing he'd ever done in his life, but it was certainly among the top five most pleasurable. Her body was driving him crazy. No, it was more than her body. It was the fire in her and the strength. She was alert at all times, always thinking, always ready for anything.

Was she ready for more than a kiss? Heaven knew he was.

Cal held a vine out of the way and let her pass. The steady wind and the sun from the cloudless sky had evaporated some of the moisture from the ground, so going back was a little less difficult than their trek to the tower had been.

He did his best to put away his carnal thoughts about Gina and focus on what they needed to do next.

She seemed busy with her own thoughts, as well. They didn't talk until they came to a point where a wide patch of fallen trees blocked the way.

"Must have been knocked down overnight by the wind," he said. It hadn't been like this on their way up.

She nodded.

"Should we go around?" He glanced at the jungle that looked pretty dense on both sides. How much time would they lose?

"Climb over."

Not an impossible task but not an easy one, either. Some trunks were three feet wide; others had fallen crisscrossing each other. If she didn't mind doing it, he could certainly keep up. He planted his boot on the first and moved forward, watching where he stepped. He extended a hand back to her to help, but she ignored it and made good progress of her own.

They had to go around the bigger branches that were sticking up, slide down to the ground, get up on the next tree trunk, over and over again. She got ahead of him at one point. Distracting. His gaze kept sliding to the efficient way she moved, feminine yet not the least hesitant. There was a quiet assurance to whatever she did, a single-minded focus, a temerity that said she'd find a way or make one.

He grinned.

Her body looked enticing from any angle. She was one of the few women who looked as good in cargo pants as she did in a bikini.

He slipped and had to grab after a branch to catch himself. "Sod it," he muttered when his foot got wedged between two sizable trees.

"Need help?" She turned to come back.

"No. Fine." He needed to stop daydreaming about her. There was something about the woman that had gotten under his skin with super speed.

He righted himself, then got going again. They were almost at the end of the obstacle course, a stretch of steep decline ahead of them that held sparse vegetation. Walking would be easier once they got that far.

She was on the last fallen tree, in the process of jumping off, when it began rolling. She couldn't jump ahead now or the tree would roll right over her.

"Cal?" She focused on staying on, doing some sort of a circus act. She couldn't jump off forward, but she couldn't jump back, either, as it seemed that first log had been holding the one behind it that was now following. Had she fallen, she would have been ground up between the two.

"Hang in there." His log was moving now, too. The first one had started a domino effect. Great. Soon a dozen trees were rolling downhill at a frighteningly steep angle, picking up speed as they went.

They couldn't stay on for more than a few seconds. The going was too bumpy as the trees flattened the low brush before them. If they fell, they would be crushed.

He looked up just in time to catch a glimpse of a washout up ahead where water running down the hill had removed the soil. Was it big enough for the both of them? What other chance did they have? "See that?"

"I'm going for it." Gina leaped as if she'd practiced this before.

His heart stopped as she disappeared in the hole.

He was only a few yards behind her. Closer, closer now. He dropped, seeing her eyes go wide as he crashed toward her, then the next log smacked him in the back of the head and pushed him into the crevice, right on top of her. He saw stars, closed his eyes against them and the sudden dizziness.

The rest of the logs thundered over them in a

rush, the whole nightmare lasting less than a minute. But it had been a nerve-shaking minute, his back taking a nasty pounding.

"I think we're okay to get out," she said under him, sounding breathless.

"Give me a minute." His head was swimming. He needed to get his bearings. "Wouldn't have minded skipping that."

"I can't breathe."

"Right. Sorry about that." He pulled up and away. "Are you all right?"

"I'm not about to complain. With a little less luck, I could have been a human pancake. You?"

He lifted a hand to the back of his head where a sizable bump was already forming. His fingertips came away bloody. "I think the logs won this round."

"Let's not go another."

"You can't fight Mother Nature." He climbed out, doing his best not to trample on her.

"Let me take a look."

"No big deal."

She flashed him an impatient glare. "Save that stiff British upper lip for another day."

As a matter of fact, he was saving his lips for her.

He didn't think she would appreciate a declaration like that, so he simply rolled his eyes at her insistence to take a look at the wound. Lord, that made him dizzy. Frankly he would have preferred to remain macho and indestructible in her eyes. Well, that ruse was up. He turned to let her look her fill.

"I could try and bring one of the four-wheelers up here."

With the logs blocking the path now? Hardly. And he wasn't hurt that badly, anyway. "I'm happy to report that my legs are in fine working order."

"You wanna be stubborn about this?"

"Absolutely." At least the dizziness was passing. The back of his head throbbed, but he was prepared to ignore that.

"Want to hold on to me?"

He grinned, torn between taking any excuse to touch her and preserving some manly image. Bad enough he'd been too stunned to enjoy the two of them being pressed together in that crevice. He promised himself to be fully operational next time they were sandwiched against each other. "I'll be fine. Thanks."

"Suit yourself."

He strode forward with purpose, just to show her that he could.

"So tell me about this Jimmy." He'd been itching for the story since the day before. He was beginning to like her. He wanted to know what he was getting himself into.

She looked at him with a guarded expression, trying to hide her surprise.

"You talk in your sleep."

"Nothing to tell." She quickened her pace.

"What did he do to you?" He did his best to catch up.

"Nothing."

"So this guy's walking down the street…he didn't look good to you, so you popped him? Let me know when I start to annoy you."

"Now."

"I like your sense of humor," he said. "I take it Jimmy didn't?"

"He—" she took a deep breath and turned enough to fix him with a glare "—beat his wife and kids senseless every single day of his miserable life."

The smile slid off his face. "The law couldn't protect them?"

Her movements became more forceful, more jerky, as if every muscle wound tight in her body. "I was the law. I couldn't do anything when everyone kept claiming all the bruises came from accidents."

She went over the next log without saying more.

"And?"

"There's no and. I don't talk about this stuff."

He glanced at his palm, which was starting to burn, and picked out a two-inch sliver without slowing. "Scared you that much?"

"He didn't scare me," she said, tight-lipped with a flash of heat in her eyes.

"Not him. That you took him out. Is that why you're no longer a cop? You quit over this?"

She ignored him for a while. Then, when he'd given up hope for an answer, she said, "I went to prison over this."

That brought him up short. "Does my cousin—"

"I'm sure he knows. It's part of why I've been recruited. The unbreakable cover. I'm a bona fide criminal." Her voice held a tinge of bitterness.

"But you were a cop," he said after a moment of reflection. "He was a wife and child abuser."

"Excessive force. The jury saw it as manslaughter."

"Nice justice system you have."

She shrugged but after a few steps stopped and looked back at him. And then it all came out.

"It wasn't the first time or the second that the neighbors called me to the house. The mother had fresh bruises. The kids were too skinny, as always, the two-year-old with a cast on his foot. Fell out of his crib, supposedly. They lost a child the year before. Fell down the stairs. They gave me the same story every time. Neighbor should mind his business. They were loud—so what? TV was on, whatever. The father was drunk or high or both. I walked through and saw a gun cabinet—new. He got a job as a two-bit security guard somewhere and weaponed up."

"Gun-happy lot, you Yanks." Which was hardly her fault, and the observation wasn't particularly helpful at the moment, either. "Never mind." He flashed her an apologetic smile. "So what happened?"

"I saw the future in that gun cabinet. Knew what I was going to find the next time I got called out." She shook her head, looking away from him.

"I asked him for registration on the weapons. I figured he had them, but I wanted him to know I was keeping a close eye on him. He got all agitated, called me a couple of choice names. The wife got the papers. She wanted me out of there, didn't want me to upset him, knew he would take it out on her and the kids when I left. I suppose I goaded him a little. I wanted him to lose it—lose it with me, with someone who could handle him for a change. He swore at the wife. I pushed him down on the chair. Guess he wasn't used to that." She cleared her throat.

He came closer to stand next to her.

"When I turned, he swung at me from behind. I blocked. He grabbed the bread knife from the table."

"So it was self-defense."

She looked him in the eye. "I could have disarmed him. See? Loyalty is a tricky thing. I was loyal to the people I was supposed to protect, as opposed to being loyal to the law. Life is one big gray area, if you ask me."

He could see the guilt in her gaze, that she lived with it still.

"If not self-defense, then defense of the family."

She flashed a tight, bitter smile. "The widow made him out to be a saint at my trial. He was bad, but he was all she had. She hated me for what I did." She started moving forward.

"Would you do it again?"

She thought about it. "I don't know. I want to think I wouldn't. That I would be smart enough to find a better way. I had too much rage." She stopped again.

"Don't beat yourself up over it. I'm feeling a lot of outrage on the issue just by listening."

She moved on in silence, her head down.

"You probably saved lives with what you've done," he told her.

She stopped and took a deep breath, blew it out. "I'm not even sure it was all about them." She looked miserable.

"You didn't shoot the guy for self-gratifica-tion. He was no threat to you. You could have walked away. You gave up your career to save that family."

She wouldn't look at him as she began walking again, keeping her attention on the ground in front of her. He supposed it had to be hard on her, even though in her profession she'd probably been prepared for the possibility that a deadly confrontation could happen. Still, from what he understood, that was rare. Most cops retired without ever having to draw their weapons. In England, the average constable didn't even carry a firearm.

He would have liked to ask more questions but figured she was done with the subject and didn't want to push her. But after a few minutes she looked back at him and began talking again.

"When I was a kid, we had a neighbor—Janie. She was my best friend. Then when she was about nine she started acting funny. Being scared of her father and whatever. She knew about sex and all long before any of us other girls. Sometimes she had bruises she wouldn't talk about." She paused.

He had a sick feeling he knew where this story was going.

"She died over Christmas break." Gina kicked a stone with her boot. "Fell down the basement stairs. I didn't put two and two together until much later. I think when I saw those kids hovering at the edge of the kitchen, stiff with fear as they watched their father, I saw Janie, too." She blinked rapidly a couple of times as she turned from him again.

"For what it's worth, I think I would have done the same," he said.

"Didn't make any difference, anyway." She shook her head, and he caught a look of vulnerability on her face that made him want to reach out to her.

He liked when she was tough and spunky but sensed that there was another side to her, one that maybe that tough shell had been developed to hide. He was seeing her other face now and it touched something inside his chest.

He held back, unsure if she would accept comfort from him. She was talking to him, taking him into her confidence. He didn't want to bring about any awkwardness between them, afraid that whatever he did might dispel the mood.

"A friend of mine from the force kept an eye on the family for me for a while," she explained. "Two months after I'd gone away, the wife shacked up with another loser, same type as the one before. She was stuck in a cycle she couldn't get out of and her kids were stuck in there with her. She wouldn't go to a shelter, wouldn't take any offered help. It was the only life she knew, the only one she felt comfortable with."

"You can't help people against their will." It

was a lesson he'd learned while trying to deal with some difficult employees.

She nodded. "There is a line. I didn't see it clearly and I crossed it."

"You served time for it." Which, in his opinion, was more than enough atonement. But it meant nothing if Gina didn't feel the same. The crux of the matter wasn't whether others could forgive her. "You should forgive yourself," he said.

The next hour or so passed mostly in silence as she was likely mulling over her past, and he tried to digest all that he'd found out about her. What she'd done and the fact that she'd been to prison didn't bother him a bit. He was a businessman with a pretty good sense for measuring people up. Gina Torno was one of the good ones.

THEY DIDN'T REACH THE four-wheelers until late in the afternoon.

"We should have brought horses." There were at least two dozen on the island, higher up from the beach, on the grassy area where Joseph Towers had stables and a corral set up. "Could have spared some walking," she said, still embarrassed that she'd told Cal about her past. There was something about him— They clicked, which was rare for her with anyone outside her sizable family.

She hadn't even talked to the others on the

team about Jimmy, and they'd become pretty close friends over the course of the mission. And yet they'd accepted her without explanations. Nothing short of a miracle, now that she thought about it. She appreciated the newfound friendships even more.

Cal wouldn't look at her.

Did her admission bother him more than he'd admitted? "What is it?" If that was the case, she would prefer to know.

"I don't care for horses."

A second passed before the meaning of his words reached her brain. The weight on her chest lifted a little. It wasn't about her past. She couldn't help but smile. But the look on his face— "Are you scared of them?" Big, bad British spy boy scared of a harmless animal? Ha.

"I'm uncomfortable around them."

He looked genuinely embarrassed, so she didn't have the heart to pick on him. "That's okay." She'd been born and raised in the city, had never been anywhere close to one. Maybe she was scared of them, too, and she just didn't know it. "No big deal."

If he could look over the fact that she'd killed someone, she could certainly forgive his reluctance to ride.

"Easy for you to say." He pressed his lips

together. "Horses. I'm British. It's like not liking Pimm's—practically treason." But he grinned.

She liked that about him, that he didn't take life too seriously. He did what he had to but didn't get hung up on things. Actually, that wasn't the only thing she liked about him. She liked his easy strength, too. That he spoke what was on his mind, straight up. She thought of the way he'd kissed her. Yet another thing she liked about the man.

"I'll go report back to Mark when we reach the shore."

"I'll update my team."

"Don't forget we're going fishing first thing in the morning," he said just as they reached a high point that was barren of trees and gave them a view below.

She could see the bungalows and the utility buildings, the small marina. The yacht was gone. So were the motorboats, the dock empty.

He was staring at that, too.

She hoped whoever had taken the yacht and the boats was coming back in a hurry.

Could their luck be this bad?

They finally had some information—earlier than she had expected—but now they were stuck on the island.

Chapter Six

"So it's a virus and it's here," Gina said, summing up the information she'd gained on the mountain.

"We figured the virus part," Carly said. "I chatted up the younger doc. They work in oncology at the moment with oncological viruses—viruses that prefer cancer cells. They are both top experts in virology, recruited by a pharmaceutical firm for research on an anticancer vaccine, then ended up at a major experimental oncology clinic."

They were gathered in the kitchen once again, just as they used to at the office—except everything had escalated a thousandfold since. And this time they were cut off from Law and Tarasov, had no one for backup.

Gina nodded. "Two expert virologists. Makes sense." She reached for another piece of chicken satay the others had saved for her from dinner and dipped it into the peanut sauce. "The virus is locked up tight."

"Should I give it a try?" Sam asked. "Not that I know that much about bank safes…Anita?"

"Just because I worked in a bank once doesn't mean I know how to break into the safe. I was nowhere near it. I did office work."

"Cal couldn't do it even with his superspy tools," Gina added, pulling the last piece of meat off, then setting aside the bamboo skewer.

"Gadgets?" Carly perked up.

Gina couldn't help a smile. "You'd like his stuff. Ask him to show you his watch when we have a quiet moment."

"Doubt we'll have many of those. We're at the finish line," Sam remarked, tugging on an eyebrow ring as she tended to do when she was nervous. "Can't believe we made it this far."

"We still don't have a location on Tsernyakov," Carly said. "I got into Mark's computer while you were gone, but it's all business stuff. Nothing in there that I could directly link to Tsernyakov's movements. Wish I could have e-mailed Brant, but I didn't dare. I don't know what security systems they have in place. The PC is linked to a server somewhere. I'm thinking off-site. I can figure out what's on the PC, but not what screens and alarms they have on the server. Too risky to keep going."

"We're not professionals. They couldn't expect us to be able to fake it all the way to the end." Sam blew the air out of her lungs.

Anita nodded in agreement. "Our makeshift training was bound to run out. Are you absolutely sure we can trust Spencer?" she asked for about the fourth time since Gina had brought the women up to date.

"What do your cop instincts say?" Sam asked.

"That he's okay." Her instincts as a woman, however, were screaming that he was so much better than that. She couldn't forget that kiss. The memory of it was enough to make her lips tingle. She pressed them together.

"Too spicy?" Anita asked, gesturing toward the peanut sauce.

"Mmm." Gina nodded and tried in vain to push Cal out of her mind.

He relit a fire in her that she'd let go out a long time ago. At the worst possible time, of course. What else was new? The men in her life tended to have lousy timing, culminating in her ex-husband, who had stuck to her like glue and demanded kids when she was a rookie cop with an overloaded and impossible schedule, then moved on to have an affair with a client of his just when she'd sorted out work and was ready to start a family.

"Let's put together what we have so far." Anita

rolled out the handmade map where they had marked all the structures on the island with copious notes about function and security.

Gina cleared the dishes and washed her hands before sitting back down to look over the map one more time. She had marked the path they'd taken up the mountain as soon as she'd gotten back, along with the tower, the bunkers and the helipad. "Anything else to add?" she asked the others. They'd been busy around the bay and the stables while she'd been gone.

They all shook their heads one by one. Whatever they had, they'd marked on the map already. The next large sheet showed layouts of buildings, the guest bungalows, the main building with the kitchen and dining room, the utility buildings. She added the approximate blueprints of the bunkers, as well, then took several pictures with her camera ring.

"Is this as complete as we can make it?" Anita looked around.

They all knew what hinged on this operation. When the commando team came in, this makeshift map would be crucial to the success of the mission.

"We got in everywhere we could," Carly said.

Gina snapped more pictures.

"Okay." Anita rolled up the papers, then handed

them to Gina. "Take them to Cal and see what he can add. As soon as Mark brings the yacht back, you two can go to Hariumat and, once you make contact, give the information to Brant." Her tone was wistful. She probably wouldn't have minded being Brant's contact person. She was soppy in love with the man.

But since it was Gina who'd seen the bunkers, she was the one with the firsthand information on the virus and Cal. She tucked the papers under her tank top, making sure they were all smoothed out and wouldn't form a bump, wouldn't stick out anywhere. The empty marina caught her gaze as she turned and shook her head.

Apparently one of the doctors had had to go back to L.A. to assist at a private patient's medical emergency. The chopper pilot had had a rough day and had been passed out, under the influence, so Mark had taken the doctor to the nearest airport, in Papeete, on the yacht. He was expected back by morning.

The large motorboat was over at Hariumat, taken out by one of the staff for grocery shopping. The small one had been pulled out of the water and was in the shop, since the wind the night before had slammed it against the pier too hard and damaged the bottom.

"I'm off to find Cal." Gina moved toward the door.

"And we'll finish the weapon inventory," Carly said.

They'd started making a list of the people on the island who had weapons that they'd seen—never openly but as bulges under shirts—and who didn't. They were also trying to discover where weapon caches were scattered.

"I'll ask Cal what he knows about the weapon situation on the island." She hadn't thought of that while they'd been together on the mountain. There were too many things to keep in mind.

She stepped outside and scanned the beach for him, holding her breath as she was hit by the beauty of the setting sun over the ocean. There were a handful of people on the beach, going about their business, one guy carrying a stack of lumber.

Cal's tall, muscular figure wasn't hard to spot. He was talking to one of Tsernyakov's men. Gina pushed away the flash of doubt that surfaced. She had to believe him. They needed him. If he was the enemy, he could have tried to take her out on the mountain. And if he'd betrayed them since they'd gotten back from the mountain, her team would be at the bottom of the ocean by now.

He wore nothing but wet swim trunks. He'd been out in the water. The setting sun glinted off his skin, playing on the muscles of his back. She wished she'd come earlier so they could have gone for a swim together. She usually did that with Anita, Carly and Sam in the mornings, but this morning she'd been at the tower, assisting Cal.

She walked toward him, enjoying the view. After what she'd been through the last couple of years, she deserved that much. It wasn't as if she intended to take the tentative alliance between them any further. He was nice to look at. She had nothing wrong with her eyes. End of story.

He finished the conversation with the other man as she neared, then walked toward her. "Having fun?"

She simply smiled. The other man stopped within hearing distance to kick off his sandals and started stretching. Looked as though he'd decided to enjoy a late-day swim, as well.

"Ask me to your room," she mouthed to Cal, too impatient to wait for the guy to go into the water.

The corner of his eyes crinkled. "Patience, luv. I was getting around to that," he said suggestively as if she weren't simply playing a part.

She glared at him, but it couldn't have been too effective considering she couldn't hold back a smile.

He gathered her close and brushed his lips against hers. *It's all for show. Nothing to get excited about,* she told herself, but it was too late. Heat zinged through her body. He pressed closer, his chest coming in contact with the papers under her shirt. They crinkled. One eyebrow slid up slightly. "Got something for me?"

"Oh, do I ever," she said in her most dangerous voice. "And as soon as we're behind closed doors, you're going to get it." It really was unfair that he could undo her so effortlessly.

He laughed. "I like a woman who puts it all on the line. No false modesty." His arms tightened around her.

And then the playful look was gone from his eyes, replaced by enough heat to scorch her eyelashes. Her mouth went dry. His gaze dropped to her lips. Her knees wobbled in anticipation. Where was the steel core she'd been relying on all these years? She didn't have time to look for it. The next second he wiped her mind clean with a thorough kiss.

HE'D MEANT TO PLAY with her a little, show off for whoever was watching, so when he took her hand and led her to his quarters it would look believable. Everyone knew they'd spent the night together on the mountain. He figured it wouldn't take much to complete that picture so that if they spent extra time in each other's company no one would find it suspicious.

But then he got lost in her scent and her eyes, in the feel of her in his arms. Kissing her didn't have a thing to do with maintaining their cover.

She tasted like peanuts. Above the sheets of paper she was hiding, her breasts pressed against him through the thin material of her tank top, her nipples hardening, poking into his naked chest. It drove him a little crazy. He deepened the kiss and left nothing of her undiscovered, took everything she had.

There was a live-wire connection between them that shot off sparks if they came anywhere near each other. At least sparks in him. It frustrated him that she seemed to be able to maintain better control than he could. *She* wasn't going around grabbing him every chance she got. Unfortunately.

His fingers spread on her back, frustrated by the tank top that stood between them. He wanted her skin against skin, eyes glazed and back bowed as he filled her. The image took the air out of his lungs and replaced it with fire instead. He pulled away reluctantly, grabbed her hand and strolled in the direction of his bungalow when what he wanted was to make love to her in the sunset right on the sand.

"What do you have?" he asked once the door was closed behind them. He needed to find some self-control and fast. He could not get so wrapped up in her that he would forget about his mission.

She pulled a wad of papers from under her shirt. Were her hands just a little unsure? His muscles tightened at the sight of her flat, tanned stomach.

His fingertips itched to discover all that soft skin. He focused on the drawings instead.

"This is what we know so far." Her voice was gratifyingly unsure. "We were wondering if you had anything to add."

"I already passed a rough map on to my connection." But he looked over her surprisingly thorough map of the island anyway. Considering the women had been here barely a few days, they had certainly been busy. He picked up a pen from the counter and made a few corrections, then moved on to the blueprints of the buildings.

"We'll hand this over, too. The more information they have the better." When he was done with the edits, he recorded each sheet of paper with his camera pen. Then he rolled them up, took them to the stove and turned on a burner, lit them, walking the burning sheets to the toilet. He changed into dry shorts and a T-shirt while he was in the bathroom.

"I should go," she said when he walked back out.

"Let's talk about tomorrow." He wasn't ready to let her go. It was a pleasure just to watch her.

"We go as soon as Mark brings back the yacht," she said with a what-is-there-to-talk-about shrug, but she stayed where she was.

"How about a drink?" He headed toward the kitchen.

"Stirred not shaken?" She grinned.

"Whatever you want." And he didn't just mean the drink.

"Mango juice would be fine."

"Great. Now how am I supposed to get you drunk and have my way with you?"

"Cal, I—" She'd come after him into the kitchen.

He handed her a glass. "Try this." He didn't want her to finish the sentence, which was bound to be some explanation about why the two of them together wasn't a good idea.

Bloody hell, he knew that. They had little in common. They had different goals in life on different continents. She probably wanted a husband and kids to get going on the whole family thing she'd missed out on while she'd been in prison. He was never going to marry again. His first wife had left him flayed when she quit. Not an experience a sane man cared to repeat.

But couldn't they just play along for the moment?

"I've never met a woman to whom I had this kind of an instant gut reaction. I'm keen on exploring it a bit further." Why wasn't she? "What would be the harm?" There, he'd laid his cards on the table.

"Your timing sucks."

"Somebody is waiting for you back home?" His jaw clenched tight at the thought.

"My family. No significant other, if that's what you're getting at."

"It was." He stepped closer.

"We shouldn't be doing this," she said but didn't back away, which gave him hope.

"Give me one good reason why."

"We're on a dangerous mission."

"What if we're killed tomorrow? We could make a hell of a last memory tonight."

She grinned and shook her head. "Does that work in British pubs? Somehow I remember double-oh-seven being smoother."

"You're throwing me off my game," he admitted, wanting to be frightfully clever and not quite managing. She took away his ability to think. "You're beautiful."

"That's supposed to be a smoother line? Not very creative." She drew up an eyebrow, not looking impressed.

He let his voice drop when he said, "I'm thinking about a number of exceedingly creative things I would like to do with you tonight."

Her eyes went wide. Was that heat flashing across her face?

He reached for her shoulders, then let his hands slide down her arms, along the silky naked skin, until he reached her hands and could hold them.

The sound of footsteps on crushed stone came

through his open window, drawing his attention. He glanced out, hating to have to take his gaze from her.

"Sergey." He nodded toward the man who was heading for the women's bungalow, glancing around surreptitiously at the now-empty beach.

"What does he want?" she asked when he stopped by their front window and looked in.

"Who's home?"

"Nobody. The others are trying to figure out what the weapon situation is. I was going to ask you about it. If you know how much there is and where the stash is kept."

"I know some," he said, keeping his eye on the man. It was hard to make out what he was doing from this distance. "We'd better go and see what he's up to," he said and headed for the door.

They kept to the shadows and found coverage in an old-fashioned wooden changing booth that was close enough to the women's bungalow to keep an eye on the man. Trouble was, the walls started a good foot and a half off the ground. Sergey would see their feet if he looked that way. The bench wasn't wide enough for them to sit side by side with their legs pulled up, the booth not tall enough for them to stand on the bench.

He got up anyway, bending deeply. The wood creaked. They held their breaths.

"Come on," he whispered.

"Where?" She looked at him bewildered.

He extended a hand and helped her up. "Turn."

She stood with her back to him now.

"Lean forward and you should be able to see out through the gap above the door."

She did, grabbing the top of the door for support. He put an arm around her waist to make sure she didn't fall.

"What do you see?" he asked, desperately trying to ignore her behind, which was pressed against his pelvic region in an intimate position.

"He's going in through the bathroom window we left open. Should we go after him and surprise him?"

He thought about that for a moment. "We'll see afterward what he touched. I don't want him to know that we're on to him." It never hurt to have an ace up one's sleeve.

He only hoped Gina didn't notice what else he had up.

Which she was bound to do if she kept moving to see better.

"Anything?" he asked after a minute, wishing he could see out, too, and had something else to focus on other than the proximity of their bodies.

"Still in there. What do you think he's doing— hiding bugs?"

"We'll do a thorough check after he leaves." Had Mark become suspicious of the women while Cal had been gone with Gina? "Did the others run into any trouble while we were up the mountain?"

"They didn't say anything." She turned to him. "I got the impression that everything went well."

"Maybe he's a kleptomaniac." He focused all his energies on picturing Sergey and what he could be doing inside the building. Not an easy task when his mind pulled full force in the direction of explicit Gina fantasies. Like what would happen if he ground himself into her from behind, if he slid a hand under her shirt and ran his fingers up her soft, warm skin to her breasts.

Her scent filled his nostrils, flooded his brain. There was no way to turn from her in the small enclosure. His thumb twitched on her slim waist.

"He's coming," she said.

Good for him.

They held their breath as Sergey passed by the cabana, going back toward his own quarters the way he had come. He didn't have anything in his hands, no telltale bulges under his clothes, either, that would have indicated he'd taken something.

When he passed out of sight, Gina jumped to the ground. "Let's check the place out."

He followed, grateful for the darkness that gave him a chance to adjust himself. He put a restraining hand on her shoulder as she reached out to put her key in the lock.

"Hold on a second. Let's move with the assumption that he was here to rig the place with explosives."

She froze for a second before she countered. "He didn't look like he was carrying anything, in or out."

"Always prepare for the worst-case scenario," he said, passing on one of the tenets of his SIS training. "The door could be booby-trapped."

She thought about that. "We'll go in the same way he did."

He nodded and rounded the building.

"Here." He held his hands out, fingers linked, for her when they got to their destination.

She stepped up, grabbed the windowsill, then pulled herself higher, brushing against him on the way. At one point his face was pressed into her abdomen. He clenched his jaw and tried not to inhale any more of her scent—soap and sun-kissed skin—that made him want to rip her shirt off with his bare teeth.

After she disappeared inside, he jumped up and grabbed the sill, worked himself over the ledge. Since he was a head taller, the job was easier for him.

She was standing still where she had landed, surveying the place.

"Anything obviously out of place?" He mouthed

the words, mindful of possible listening devices. He hadn't been inside the bungalow since the women had arrived. The living room looked like a traveling fashion show, clothes scattered around on the furniture.

She gave it some time before she responded. "Nothing that I can spot from here," she mouthed back.

He passed her and checked for hidden explosives first, any sign of odd wiring. When he didn't find any, and was sure turning a switch wouldn't set anything off, he flicked on the light. He gave her a thumbs-up and they moved to search for bugs.

"Clear," she said after a good half hour.

"Same here." He closed the last kitchen cabinet. "I couldn't find anything missing downstairs. Let's check above."

She moved up the stairs and he followed, taking the first door to the left while she took the one to the right. Anita's room; he recognized her clothes. The room was tidy, much more so than the common area below. Nothing looked out of place, nothing looked as if it had been touched. He moved on to the next room—Gina's.

The air carried her subtle scent, assailing him as soon as he opened the door. Everything was orderly here, as well, making him wonder if Sam and Carly were the messy ones in the group. He went to the closet first, then the dresser, skirting her bed. Nothing looked as if it had been searched through. He pulled open one dresser drawer after the other, his hand stopping in midmotion, his brain blanking as he got to the one that was filled with tidy rows of silk underwear.

She was an ex-cop. Couldn't she wear sensible cotton? He couldn't stop himself from picturing her in the array of colors in front of him.

"Find anything interesting?" she asked from the door.

He slammed the drawer shut and turned. God, she was beautiful. "Plenty, but maybe you should look. You'd know better what things looked like before." He backed away, banging the back of his knees against the bed, and had a sudden vision of the two of them tangled in the sheets.

"You okay?"

I want you so much I can't breathe, was the first thing that popped into his mind. Instead of saying it, however, he escaped out the door.

She was one of the most beautiful and intelligent women he'd ever met. There was nothing wrong with being attracted to her, he told himself as he padded down the stairs. He just didn't like how out of control the attraction was getting.

He grabbed a soda from the fridge and leaned

against the counter, letting his gaze skim the area around him as he drank. What had Sergey been doing in here?

Gina was coming down the stairs. "Can't find a thing out of place."

"I'll go pay Sergey a visit before we take the boat out in the morning. I don't feel comfortable leaving your friends here alone with Sergey sneaking in and out."

She drew up a sexy eyebrow as she came closer. "They're trained operatives."

"I'm a gentleman."

She just about gaped at him, the look on her face making his lips twitch.

She thought for a moment, her gaze hardening. "Let's make one thing clear. You're not taking over our operation just because you're a man. We'll cooperate as equals." She emphasized the last word.

"It turns me on when you get all tough on me," he said and stepped forward, self-control be damned.

He could run from the stunning strength of his attraction, but what good would that do? He'd had his share of women before his marriage and since his divorce. He knew how to have fun without getting involved. Although the circumstances were far from ideal, it was better to neutralize the distraction rather than allow it to mess him up and maybe mess up the operation in turn.

He'd made his decision in that split second. The next, she was snugly enfolded in his arms.

Her eyes went wide, and for a moment he felt as if he could fall into those golden pools. Then he reminded himself that double-oh-seven didn't fall. So he moved ahead and conquered.

WHO DID HE THINK HE was?

His infuriating habit of kissing her whenever the mood struck him had to be stopped. He had to be shown who was in control. She pressed her body hard up against him, making sure he felt every curve, and kissed him back, giving as good as she got.

And soon realized that she was dueling with a master.

He dropped his hands to cup her behind. She dropped hers until the hard muscles of his buttocks filled them. And then she pulled him even closer.

The proof that she was having a definite effect on him was gratifying.

He lifted her up and she wrapped her legs around him on reflex. Then he was moving her toward the counter, depositing her on it. Good thinking—her knees were getting wobbly anyway.

Did it give him the upper hand that his weren't? She slid her hands under his shirt, exploring the hills and valleys of smooth skin over muscles, to make sure he knew she was far from capitulation. His nipples hardened as she brushed over them.

His body was perfectly built and proportioned. She gave herself over to the enjoyment of it. She deserved that much after all the years of solitude. He was offering and she had half a mind to accept. What harm could it do? They could enjoy each other's bodies for a few days, then part ways, no strings, no regrets.

Could she do it?

She'd tried commitment and that hadn't worked. Maybe she was a better fit for a no-strings deal. His hands came around to cup her breasts, and her body hummed in approval.

He was the perfect casual relationship: hot as all get-out, straightforward, a confirmed bachelor, possessing a body that would make any red-blooded woman weep for joy. And when they were done he would be an ocean away, making it unlikely that they would ever run into each other again, giving rise to regrets or embarrassment.

He opened her front-closure bra with a flick of his thumb.

Smooth. She appreciated that at the moment, the breath catching in her throat as her breasts tumbled forward into the heat of his waiting palms. She highly approved of the way his lips trailed down from her mouth, heading in the perfect direction. She leaned back and let her head drop, allowing him free rein of her neck, bit back a moan when his wet mouth closed over one of her nipples through the thin material of her tank top.

She was going to mount a counteroffensive in a minute. She just had to gather her thoughts first, let him exhaust himself a little. There seemed to be a problem with serious mental haze, however. Especially when he pulled her shirt over her head, removing the bra with it in one easy move.

But she still wasn't ready to capitulate. There was fight in her yet. She slid a hand between them and cupped his hardness.

Impressive.

And in that split second she could feel what it would be like for him to slide inside her. Her pulse quickened. He was rubbing her with the palm of his hand in a slow circular motion. She felt her body tighten and felt powerless to stop the tide.

He lifted his head from her breasts, and she caught a look of fierce concentration on his face as he watched her. And she knew she was going to lose this battle.

He claimed her lips again at the exact moment when her body convulsed and spirals of pleasure swirled through her. She collapsed against his chest, holding on for support.

She didn't have much time to gather her thoughts.

"Interrupting anything?" The question came from the door. Carly was standing over the threshold with a self-satisfied smirk on her face, her eyes firmly fixed on her feet.

Gina cringed even though Cal was covering her with his body. Still, it had to be pretty obvious what they were doing. Her heart hammered against her chest, her body weak from her release. She couldn't come up with a good explanation. She couldn't utter a single word.

Carly didn't seem to need one. "Keep up the good work," she said as she backed out, wiggling her eyebrows suggestively. "I forgot my bag at the tiki bar. Mind walking back with me?" she called out. Apparently the others were behind her on the path.

Chapter Seven

"So we think there's an extra room upstairs," Anita said, after Cal had left and the other women had returned to the bungalow.

"How big of an area are we talking about?" Gina asked, grateful that none of the women mentioned her being caught with Cal. She was confused on the issue enough already. She couldn't possibly explain something to others that she herself didn't yet understand. What had she been thinking?

"Not much, maybe three or four hundred square feet. I've spent a lot of time in the kitchen lately, and when I was looking around upstairs last night, I started to compare the square footage with the area below. It's definitely not a match." Anita rubbed her temple.

She looked tired. They all did. They were working their plan every minute of the day, learning as much as they could about the place, knowing every piece of information would be vital when the commando team got here.

"So when do we go back?" Gina asked, relieved to have something to focus on other than how her body still tingled from pleasure.

"We were thinking about doing it before dawn." Carly sprawled in a kitchen chair. "Maybe around four? Everybody should be asleep by then."

"And the early risers should still be in bed," Anita added.

"Let's make it three." Gina wanted to make sure they were done by the time she was supposed to take the yacht out with Cal at first light. Mark had finally returned.

The others agreed.

For a moment she thought about going over to Cal and telling him about this latest development but then decided not to. She wasn't ready to be alone with him in his bungalow just now. Too many things had happened in the past few days, in the past few hours. Before she saw him again she needed to sort out a couple of things. She would just tell him the end result of their night recon tomorrow on the yacht.

To be honest, she was embarrassed to face him right now. It was so unlike her to completely lose herself, to throw all caution to the wind. She wanted to put it down to the adrenaline-charged atmosphere, but she'd been in plenty of highly charged situations on the police force and had never behaved like this.

And, yes, she'd been alone for a long time, but she would have had plenty of opportunities on Grand Cayman to hook up with a man and ease her loneliness. The team had attended plenty of cocktail parties and receptions as part of their cover. She had gotten a number of offers. And she'd turned down each and every one.

So why did Cal Spencer get to her where others couldn't?

THERE WERE ARMED men on the beach, two that she could see, guarding the island from intruders on the water. Mark had recommended that the guests stay inside late at night. He played down the presence of the guards, saying something about a negligible possibility of pirates getting out of hand—which, he assured them, never happened, but better safe than sorry.

The four women put on dark clothes, turned a light on in the living room in the front and turned on the TV—as if one of them was having trouble sleeping—hoping if anyone glanced toward the bungalow, their attention would be drawn by the light and the muffled sounds of late-night programming. Then they sneaked out through a back window.

They crept from bush to bush, skittering forward across the gaps, keeping low and communicating with hand signals only. When they were off the beach and in the cover of vegetation, they moved parallel to shore until they were in line with the main building. Unlike the other structures, which stood on posts and were made of wood, this had a cement base and brick walls.

Gina ran her gaze down the length of the backside. She'd noticed the differences on arrival but figured it was the safe house for guests and staff in the event of cyclones, which, from what she'd heard from Mark, weren't uncommon in the region.

"Here we go." Anita sneaked forward, ran across the sand and, when she reached the back wall, pushed a small window open.

She was a regular visitor in the kitchen, pretending that nothing interested her more than French Polynesian cooking. She had mapped the area and set up their entry the evening before. Apparently nobody had checked the windows when they'd locked up the place for the night. Looked as though the staff relaxed their standards while the boss was away. Sam had been prepared with her tool kit, but this way their entry would be quicker and easier.

"Let's move," she said and went next, leaving

Gina and Carly alone behind the big-leafed fernlike bush.

"About this evening…" Gina whispered, clearing her throat. "Thanks for not saying anything."

Carly looked at her for a long moment. "I hope it'll work for you. But if it turns out he's not on our side and he's just playing with you—" a fierce expression stole onto her face "—he's going to seriously have to answer to us."

"Damn right." Gina grinned. It was nice to have someone watch her back, to have friends who cared about her and watched out for her. The grin faded as she thought of Cal. "I'm not in love with him or anything. It's—" She drew a deep breath. "I don't know what it is. Pure chemistry. I've never seen anything like this before. I'm confused out of my mind, which doesn't seem to stop me from wanting him."

"He's pretty hot," Carly conceded before she sneaked inside after Sam.

Yes, he was hot. Lust. That's what it was about. Simple lust. Gina waited until Carly reached safety, then went in after her.

They stood still in the silence of the bamboo-paneled bathroom. So far, so good. Nobody had raised the alarm.

According to their observations, the main building was deserted at night. The downstairs was taken up by the kitchen, dining room and storage rooms; the upstairs area had offices that didn't seem to be in use. Only Mark went up there now and then.

Since Anita knew the place best, she went first and the rest of them followed. The kitchen still smelled like dinner and a little bit of bleach from the end-of-day cleanup. Stainless steel appliances gleamed in the moonlight that filtered through the windows. Pots and pans hung from hooks on the walls, refrigerators hummed quietly in the night.

Bang!

Gina whipped around, holding her trusty steak knife. She needed to get her hands on a real weapon. She'd given the machete back to Cal. Couldn't very well walk around the beach with that. It wasn't the sort of thing you could hide in a skimpy pair of shorts.

"Sorry." Sam pulled her neck in, an apologetic look on her face. A bucket of taro lay kicked over at her feet.

They listened for any sound that would indicate somebody had heard them. Seconds ticked by, one after the other.

"We're okay," Gina whispered when it seemed nobody was coming to investigate.

Sam bent and straightened up the mess she'd made.

They stuck together and found the stairs without further incident. Once they were upstairs, Gina tried to keep the layout of the downstairs in mind and figure out where the hidden space was. According to Anita, it had to be on the west side. After a moment, she agreed.

Nothing there but wall. She knocked on it. Solid brick. She used her penlight to check for signs of a hidden door but found nothing. Other than the main area, a small office shared a wall with the phantom space, as well. They checked that out.

A desk and chair, file cabinets, a large metal office closet. Boxes stood piled high against the walls. While the place wasn't sparkling clean in general, the boxes didn't have any dust on them. Looked as though they'd been brought here recently. There were too many to search right now, but she opened one and pulled out some papers. Odd lettering filled the pages. Russian. She took a few pictures with her camera ring, then put everything back in place.

Carly tested the door of the office closet, rattling the knob gently to avoid making too much noise. "Locked."

Sam came forward with her tool kit and had it open in under a minute.

They weren't all that surprised to see another door in the back of the cabinet instead of shelves.

"Bingo." Carly grinned.

Sam was working on that lock already. "This one is a good one," she said.

Gina watched as she manipulated the picks like an expert, her facial muscles growing tighter and tighter, her eyes narrowed, her whole being focused on the job. But her efforts didn't bring results.

Gina glanced toward the door. If she went and got Cal, maybe he could try one of his gadgets. But then the lock popped and Sam straightened with a self-satisfied grin, and Gina put Cal from her mind.

The area they discovered was one big room with a central console and a single bed by the wall. Various screens were on, sunk into the desktop, green blips moving.

"Air and land radar," Gina said.

"Some kind of command center." Carly walked around.

Dozens of boxes were stored in here, too. Was Tsernyakov moving his operations—or parts of it—here?

Gina stepped closer to the controls and watched them for a while, compared them to the map on the wall. She could see two small ships not too far off the north of the island. Pirates? Supposedly that was their territory. A larger ship was approaching from the south, looking as though it was heading straight for shore. Odd that it wouldn't come around to the bay. What would it be doing on the other side of the island?

The bunkers.

Was Tsernyakov coming right now to retrieve the virus?

"Hey, I think—" She bit off the rest as a small noise came from behind her.

"Hands above your heads. Slowly." Mark stood in the doorway, pointing a semiautomatic at them.

She clenched her fists but controlled the need to act on the first impulse, to try to fight their way out. They'd come so far. She hated to fail now. *Hated* it.

She assessed the situation. He was alone. There were four of them. Gina gave the others a meaningful look, one by one. The second the guy's back was turned or he was distracted in any way—

"Care to tell me what you're doing here?"

There was no point trying to make up a story. They'd sneaked into the building in the dark, broken two locks to get this far. There was no innocent explanation.

"I thought so," Mark said when no response was forthcoming. "Tie them up." He stepped aside and two other men came in, armed the same.

Her knife was stuck in the back of her shorts— not that there was much she could have done with it, anyway. The guns pretty much sealed the outcome of the meeting. Better to stay alive right now so they could attempt an escape later, when the odds improved. She raised her hands along with the others, who seemed to have come to the same conclusion.

If they were to be tied up, they would be left alive for a while yet. If Mark wanted them dead this second, he could have shot them right there. Nobody was going to question him on this island.

She let Sergey tie on the nylon restraints, same as the Flex-Cufs she'd used plenty of times before on the job. At least she still had her knife. She was glad now that she hadn't pulled that at the beginning and so it had remained out of sight. Her hopes were dashed the next second when Sergey patted her down and took it, shaking his head with a leering-slash-mocking expression. She could do nothing but give him a fierce glare. She did balk, however, when he took a small black sack from his pocket and pulled it over her head.

TSERNYAKOV LOOKED OUT over the city one last time and watched the people below, who were out on the streets even this time of the night. Ignorance, indeed, was bliss. If they knew what awaited them, panic would rule.

It will. Soon. He'd be watching it on television.

A heady feeling came with the thought, with

this new level of power he wielded. *I'm the one who makes it happen.*

He'd never believed in destruction for the sake of an ideal, without monetary profit, but he got a glimpse of something now, the feeling of sheer power that went beyond money—to be the one to hold the lives of millions in the palm of his hand.

Of course, he *would* make money on the deal. A lot of it, transferred to him by the School Board within days. He understood them a little better now, but still, he wasn't the type to abandon his principles from one day to the next. He thought of what was soon to come and for a moment he got dizzy. Then, when that subsided, suddenly aroused.

He started for the chopper that waited in the middle of the roof and pictured Alexandra at his fortress of a ranch, waiting for him. He would be by her side soon.

Everything stood ready. He had an elaborate system of defense in place for the handover that was to take place in the middle of the Pacific Ocean. He had a decommissioned destroyer he'd bought off the Russian navy nearly two decades ago. Security was in place, his men keeping vigil by the hundreds.

He paused as he thought about it.

Maybe that was it, the nagging doubt he

couldn't shake. Was the plan too big to be concealed? He couldn't change it now. The date was set, everyone was ready.

Including his enemies, if he'd been betrayed.

The chopper lifted into the air and banked to the left.

His instincts had been prickling for some time, but he couldn't put a finger on what was setting off his internal alarms. He'd already ordered the execution of a half dozen men in his organization whom he hadn't been sure about, but even that failed to set his mind at ease.

He made a split-second decision. He would keep the original plan. For decoy. The handover would take place somewhere else, with as few people as possible. He needed to visit his island anyway, was expected there one of these days. That was nothing out of the ordinary. He did that from time to time. Nobody should get suspicious. A slow smile spread across his face as he leaned back in his seat and gave new instructions to the pilot.

WERE THEY ALONE FINALLY?

Gina reached for the hood on her head. From the fact that nobody kicked her in the ribs this time she surmised that their captors had left them. She pulled off the scratchy material but still couldn't see anything.

"You guys okay?"

"Yeah."

"Peachy."

"Never better," came from somewhere in the darkness.

"Where do you think we are?" Anita asked.

Gina stood and walked forward with her tied hands extended in front of her. "Sorry," she said when she bumped into a soft body.

"Just me," Sam said.

She kept going until her hands met something solid. Cardboard boxes? She went around and hit a cement wall after a few steps. "I think we're in one of the bunkers."

The realization sank any hope she had for a quick getaway. All the bunkers were fully secured. No way they could get out of here unless Cal came by and unlocked the keypad with his gadget watch from the outside. But Cal had no idea they were here. How long would it take him to realize that they were missing? Would he think of the bunkers? Would Mark tell him what had happened in the middle of the night? Would Cal come for them or would he take the yacht to his connection? The virus, no matter what, took priority.

There was a third option, too, one she didn't want to think about. Had Cal betrayed them? The thought chilled her. Was that why Mark had been keeping an eye on them and caught them breaking in? Was that why Sergey had known she had the knife?

Had Cal given in to his misguided feelings of guilt over going against family? Or had he not had any scruples at all from the beginning and all his soul-searching and doubts had been for her benefit? Could all her cop instincts fail her this spectacularly? Had she completely lost her edge while she'd been in the can?

She cringed when she thought back to the way she'd let him touch her, the way she'd given her body to him. Had she been blinded by lust? She wanted to rage and beat her head against the wall. She wanted to get her hands on him and do whatever it took to get the truth out of the man.

But there was nothing she could do about him right now. They would have to get out of here first. She thought over all that had happened that night, focusing on the blip on the radar. "I think we're about to have company."

"What are you talking about?" Carly asked from nearby.

She told them what she'd seen in the command room and what she thought of it.

"Could be more pirates." Anita attempted remaining positive.

She wished she could be like that. "This is a big boat, heading straight for this side of the island."

"But it's not the twenty-seventh yet," Sam protested.

That gave her a little hope.

Some muffled sounds came from above. She thought it was mechanical but couldn't be sure. Could be a helicopter, could be the wind in the trees. It stopped after a few seconds.

"Which bunker are we in?" Anita asked.

Gina had told the others all about the exploration she had conducted with Cal. They'd seen the blueprints she had drawn up. She nearly groaned aloud at the thought of having given all that information to Cal along with every bit of intelligence they had managed to collect since they'd been on the island. She'd figured he would be less likely to be searched. He had burned all their drawings. The urge to bang her head into the wall returned. She no longer even had her camera ring. Mark's men had stripped them of everything but their clothes.

Everything they'd worked for since they'd arrived on the island was gone.

"Are we where the virus is?" Carly asked from somewhere in the darkness.

"Let me see." Gina moved along the wall and measured the space. Better to do something, anything, than to think about Cal's possible betrayal. She didn't want to believe that he had put on an act all along. Surely not when he'd kissed her or when they'd been in the kitchen. She hated that even now her body remembered as she thought of what had happened between them— remembered and responded.

Had he seduced her to gain her trust? God, she'd been an easy mark. She'd been attracted to him from the moment they'd first fallen from the ceiling.

That thought gave her hope. He *had* been spying on Mark. She'd been there, seen it with her own eyes. What other explanation could there be? Maybe he was telling the truth and was on his way even now to save them.

And maybe she was in denial just like all those people she'd met in the course of her work who couldn't face the fact that someone they cared about could be bad. Except that she didn't care about Cal. Attracted, yes. There was nothing beyond that. It would have been madness.

She came to a large hole in the wall, the beginning of a tunnel, walled off evenly. "We're definitely not in the bunker with the virus. That was smaller and had a long tunnel in the back."

"They might not even come back here," Anita said. "They might take the virus and leave."

The thought of being left indefinitely in the tomblike space settled into her chest, a hard, cold presence, adding to the weight of Cal's possible betrayal.

"You said there were supplies in the bunkers," Carly remarked. "Maybe it's for after, when the world is in chaos. Eventually they'll come back for what they stashed here."

"Could be." Maybe Tsernyakov's men had no plans to kill them just now. If the transfer was taking place soon, they might have their hands full already. Maybe they were holding them for a leisurely torture to find out who sent them. Mark had asked precious few questions.

Maybe because he had the answers from Cal already.

She bumped into another row of boxes as she moved forward. "At least we won't die of thirst or starvation while we're waiting for them to return," she said, remembering the MREs and water jugs.

"We have to get out of here before they come for us," Sam said, stating the obvious. Judging from her voice, she was moving around, too.

"We can't get through the door," Anita said from the direction of the door. "Do you have your tool kit?" she asked Sam.

"They took it."

"You said each bunker had tunnels." Carly's voice came from the back wall now.

"All collapsed or walled in."

"Are you sure we can't dig ourselves out?"

"With what? Our bare hands?" She reached up to push a box off the top. Her throat was parched. The others had to be feeling the same.

"People did that," Sam said. "Remember the stories?"

"Tales of impossible prison escapes inmates like to entertain each other with. Even if anything like that did happen, it must have taken years." She didn't think they had more than a couple of days at best. "I'm getting something to drink," she warned so they wouldn't be startled by the crash, then pushed the box over.

It hit the floor with a loud bang.

"Where is the air coming from?" Anita asked.

Gina stopped in midmotion as she was reaching blindly for a bottle. "I don't know." She straightened. There definitely was a slight breeze. "Where do you feel it the strongest?" She moved around, rotating her face, trying to find the source of the air stream. "Sorry," she said when she bumped into someone.

"Don't worry about it," Carly said.

"Right here," Anita was calling from somewhere on her left.

She moved that way and collided with Carly again. Then they reached Anita.

"It's coming from above." Gina turned her face toward the ceiling. Cool night air streamed in a steady flow. "Makes sense that there would be a ventilation hole somewhere."

"Let's see how big it is," Carly said. "I'm the tallest. I'll be on the bottom."

"Come on, Sam." Gina turned toward the sound that came from behind her. "You're the lightest. Up you go."

Sam bumped into her. "I'm here."

"I'll help you up."

"Step into my hands," Carly said.

Sam did as she was told, and Gina pushed her, then held her feet for added support once she was standing on Carly's shoulders.

"Careful," Anita said next to them. "What do you feel?"

"An opening in the ceiling. Square."

"Can you fit through?"

"Yes."

They breathed a collective sigh of relief.

"Can you pull yourself up and see where it leads?"

"It's blocked."

"Can we get out that way?"

Sam's weight shifted as she heaved against something that made a loud scraping noise. "There's a metal grid closing off the way."

"Push as hard as you can."

"I'm doing it," Sam bit back, her voice strained, betraying the effort she put into the work. "It's not budging."

"Let me try," Gina said, frustrated and impatient. She was in pretty good shape. She got used to working out when she'd been on the force, then kept up with it in prison and even after they'd gotten out.

She helped Sam to the ground.

"Can you handle me or would you prefer to rest first?" she asked Carly.

"Let's try this," she said.

Gina grabbed on to the woman's shoulder as best she could with her hands tied together, thankful for Anita and Sam, who were pushing her from behind. They held her ankles when she was all the way up.

She found the opening in the ceiling easily and reached inside, touched the metal, shook it. Rust came away on her hands. The bars gave a little but not nearly enough. She pushed with everything she had in her but couldn't get anything beyond a minuscule movement. If her hands weren't tied, she could do better. She swore silently and tried again. The damn thing had to be up there for how many decades? The bunker had been built during WWII. Why couldn't the tropical weather have eaten through it by now? She tried again.

"I'm coming down," she said after another failure. She wanted to give Carly a break.

"Now what?" Sam asked.

"The thigh muscles are one of the strongest in the body," Carly remarked. "What if you tried upside down? Gave it a good kick?"

"Can that be done?" Anita's voice held cautious excitement.

"We won't know until we try. Let's rest a few minutes first so you can hold me for a while. I want to be able to get in as many kicks in as short a time as possible," Gina said. "Water anyone?" She went back in the direction of the box she'd busted open and searched the ground, came up with a bottle.

The others accepted the offer.

They took a three-minute break, then Carly, Sam and Anita made a group-hug-like formation and she got on top, rested her shoulders on theirs. She lifted her legs toward the ceiling, balancing carefully. Once again they supported her with their hands. The bottom of her shoes touched the ceiling before she could have straightened her feet.

"I think we've moved away from the hole." Just what they needed. "Try a little to the right."

They moved, rattling the whole circus act. Blood was rushing into her head.

No hole here, either.

"A little to the left." She felt with her feet. "There. We have it."

She extended her feet up, laid the sole of her shoes against the grid and pushed. It moved more than it had earlier. She pulled back and delivered a swift kick. Dust and bits and pieces of cement sprinkled from above, into her face. She tried to blink it out of her eyes. Shouldn't have had them open. What was the point, anyway? She couldn't see anything.

Carly coughed, rattling the precarious structure, making Gina sway.

She braced her legs against the wall to steady herself. "Try not to drop me."

"No worries. We've got you," Carly said before she coughed again.

They did, Gina realized with some surprise. She trusted these three women as though they were her own sisters. Somehow in the course of the mission they'd gone from strangers to the best partners she could wish for, to friends. She wasn't about to let them down. She kicked again and put all her heart into it.

She wasn't going to die on this stupid island. She wasn't going to let down her friends, her family and the millions of innocent people around the world that the virus would kill. She kicked.

This time the grate moved. Really moved. One side of it was a few inches higher than the other.

"It's working," she said, her throat raw from the effort and from talking upside down.

With the next kick the grate broke loose, although it felt as if it was still tangled in something. Barbed wire? Is that how bunkers worked?

"I need to feel around to see what's going on up there. I have to turn right side up again." She lowered her legs, began to fall but hands shot out to catch her. "Thanks."

They took another quick break, then the balancing act assembled again.

"When this is over, let's put together an act and go to Vegas," Carly said.

"Stop trying to make me laugh. I don't want to fall." Gina reached up through the hole, her arm getting scratched. The grate was free of its base but held down by a jumble of vines. She tore at them, thorns biting into her palms. She could feel blood trickling down her wrist.

"This is not going to work bare-handed. There are a lot of prickly things up here."

There was a moment of shuffling down below, then Anita said, "Here, take my shirt."

She reached down and wrapped the material around her right hand, then went back to work. Much better. "Thanks."

When there was sufficient room, she pulled herself up and supported herself by wedging her feet against the side of the vent hole. Then she cleared the dense vegetation enough to finally see the starry sky above.

"I'm through," she called back. She couldn't lie down near the hole, however, to reach down for the next person. The area she'd cleared in the aggressive vegetation was barely large enough for her to stand up. "There's some serious kudzu up here. Give me a second to figure out how I can help you guys up."

"You know the way back to the bay. You've been here before. Go get Cal if you can or get a boat and go around to come back for us. We'll get out," Carly said from below. "We'll meet you down at the shore."

She didn't want to tell them about her suspicions about Cal, didn't want to dash even that dim glimmer of hope. She would deal with Cal. "Okay."

She hated leaving her friends down there, but she realized that Carly was right. They had no time to waste. She tossed Anita's shirt back, broke off a thick branch to use as a makeshift hatchet and began to press her way through.

Once she got past the jumble of vines above the bunker, the rest was much easier. The area on this part of the hillside wasn't overly bushy; there were enough trees to block out most of the sunlight during the day and prevent serious undergrowth. She went in the opposite direction from the ocean. When she was no longer sure if she was still keeping the right direction, she climbed a tree.

The satellite tower was clearly visible from her perch, outlined against the dim moon in the sky. She climbed down and started toward it. It probably wasn't the shortest way to go, but from the tower there was a track to the bay, to the boats and Cal.

The night jungle was full of noises, birds startling her by crying out, then taking sudden flight, small animals skittering by among the dead leaves as she stepped. She was a city girl through and through. Frankly she found this much nature threatening. She stopped to catch her breath. It had been much easier before, when she hadn't been alone.

And then she heard another noise, one that didn't come from a mouse or a harmless forest snake. Something big was moving through the woods.

Were Mark and his men returning already?

She turned, ready to go back to warn the others. Then she hesitated. Maybe she could draw the men after herself, allowing the others enough time to get out, get away from the bunker and hide.

She moved forward and moved fast, not caring how much noise she made.

The thick canopy blocked out most of the moonlight from above. All she could see were shadows. She began to run, nearly tripped, so she slowed again. She held her breath, trying to hear if whoever else was in the woods was still following her or not, but could barely hear anything over the blood pounding in her ears.

God, she was out of practice. Where was the steely calm she could always count on when she'd been a cop? She had always been able to cope with tense situations, had never lost her cool until that one fateful day with Jimmy.

People are counting on me to protect them. I'm in control. She pictured herself in the uniform, her gun strapped to her side. And slowly she felt her old self slipping back in.

She stopped, caught the sound of footsteps. Then the sound died.

She moved forward again. She wanted the men as far from the bunkers as possible, give the others as much time as she could. But she couldn't lead those goons around in the woods forever. She needed to get to the bay and steal a boat, come around the island and pick up the rest of her team. Then they could take the boat to Hariumat and make contact with Brant. The commando team needed to get to the island ASAP.

When she thought she'd led whoever was following her far enough, she changed tactics and turned toward the bay, moving slowly and silently. It would take the men a while to realize that they'd lost her, then even more time to get back to the bunkers. She hoped the time she'd been able to gain for the others would be enough.

She was nearly at the end of the woods, could make out another semibarren area ahead. Should she try to go around? How much time would that waste? Were the men still behind her? She stopped to listen but couldn't hear any suspicious noises. She eyed the low bushes. Morning neared, but it was still pretty dark. She should be able to make it across.

But before she could take the first step, a shadow detached from the trees on her right and slammed into her hard, taking her to the ground.

Chapter Eight

"It's me." Cal had recognized her body the second he'd come in contact with it and ducked to avoid the head slam coming his way.

Gina stilled. He'd found her. He let himself relax. She took advantage of that to heave herself up and reverse their positions. What the hell—

"You betrayed us." With her hands still tied together, she couldn't pin his down.

He didn't struggle—that would have just drawn out the fight. He needed to figure out what was going on in her head and talk her into listening to him. "We don't have time for this. I have to get you out of here."

"How did Mark know about us?" Her voice was sharp.

She thought from him? That stung. But it *was* a valid question, one he hadn't had the chance to pose to the man. "Maybe Sergey found something suspicious in your place and they were watching the lot of you."

She wouldn't let up. She wasn't buying any of it.

"In the interest of time, I think you should get off," he said, exasperated, and wiggled his torso. Big mistake. His body sensed none of the danger around them, only her curves on top. And responded appropriately.

He stilled and took a deep breath. Awareness stretched between them.

"One of these days we'll get together somewhere where danger doesn't threaten every second and have some serious skin-to-skin time," he said and rolled them with a single move, planting himself squarely on top again.

"I hate this." She heaved against him.

It just aroused him further. He dipped his head. "Me, too."

"Half the time I don't know if you're going to kill me or kiss me."

"Kiss you," he said a hairbreadth away. "I haven't seriously thought about eliminating you since that first day."

"Jeez, that sets my mind at ease."

"It was unfailingly rude of me, I admit. Under the current circumstances, you must understand—"

"If you think I—"

He pressed his lips against hers, getting lost in

the relief that he'd found her alive. She capitulated too easily. Then he realized why. She was going for the gun tucked behind his back. He let her have it, then rolled off her.

"If it makes you feel better," he said.

She made a dismissing noise in her throat.

He reached for his knife. "Would you like me to cut that off?" He nodded toward the nylon restraint.

After a moment of thought, she extended her hands slowly, without taking the gun off him.

"My feelings are seriously getting hurt. A little trust would go a long way, considering we are in this together." He sawed and freed her in seconds.

She lowered the gun.

"You scared me." She was still breathing hard—from their wrestling and the fright he'd given her—and trying not to show it.

"I'm on your side. We'll make this work." He had made some plans on his way over, some plans he needed her help with and others she could know nothing about.

He stood and turned back toward the bunkers, in the direction they'd come from. "We need to get going. Where were you headed, anyway?"

She'd been moving through the jungle at a fair speed. In the dark.

Tension pulled his muscles tighter. She could have hurt herself. Bloody hell, she could have been killed by his cousin's men, for that matter, something he hadn't allowed himself to think about on his way here.

"I'm sorry I scared you." He'd been half out of his mind since he'd been woken by Mark and found out what had happened.

"What are *you* doing here?" she asked, keeping pace with him.

When she nearly tripped, he put a steadying hand to her back, just to be able to feel her again.

"I told Mark I was taking the yacht out fishing and came around the island to get you and your friends. Figured there was a good chance you were somewhere around the bunkers but heard some noise in the woods and followed it instead. Where are the others?"

"Hopefully on their way to the shore. I was going back to the bay to get a boat so I could return to pick them up." She stopped and rubbed her palm over her face. She looked exhausted. Her gaze searched his eyes. She took a slow breath, then let it out, seeming to have come to some sort of decision. "I'm glad you came."

The tension in his chest eased a little. Gina was here, unharmed. Everyone was still okay. He hadn't been too late. "I have the yacht a half a mile from the first bunker." And not a minute to waste.

"There's a ship coming in," she said as they

made quick progress now that dawn was breaking over the horizon and there was more and more light to walk by. "We got into some kind of control room and saw the radar."

"Control room?" What was she talking about?

"Above the kitchen." She gave him a brief rundown on how their night had gone and what they had found.

"Should have told me you were going." He could have provided backup or made sure Mark and his men were distracted someplace else.

"Didn't seem like a big deal at the time. I'll buy that Sergey found something or overheard something, although I can't imagine what. But what made him come snooping around us in the first place?"

"Maybe you set off some silent alarm while you were going through the place with your friends." Mark hadn't mentioned anything like that when Cal had arrived on the island and showed interest in security, but considering the control room, it looked as though Mark hadn't told him everything.

Looked as though his cousin didn't trust him completely. With good reason, he supposed.

"Silent alarm?" She looked doubtful. Probably still thought he was making all this up.

"Look…" He didn't quite manage to keep the

frustration out of his voice. "You want solid answers and certainty, things you could enter as evidence. There's none of that in this situation. We are both working blind. I barely know more than you do. The first time I talked with Joseph was a couple of months ago. I've only seen him twice. I don't know everything there is to know about the man or how he works. That's why I'm here—to find more information, to find enough so the people who recruited me can stop him."

"Okay. I get it." She held up a hand. "It's a live-wire situation. Trust is not my first instinct."

He could understand that.

They walked on.

"So we figured the ship is bringing Tsernya-kov," she said after a while.

He shook his head. "He's coming in by air. The pilot already took off in one of the choppers to pick him up. He'll be here in a couple of hours. I think he might be moving up the handover date. Could be for security, could be because of the weather." He pushed harder, picking up speed. "The cyclone is changing direction. It's not going to hit the island, but its wings are definitely going to brush us."

"Then who is coming on the ship?" Gina kept up with him as he pushed his way through vines and over fallen trees, slapping ferns out of the way.

"I'm guessing the buyers." The thought of a boatload of terrorists arriving on the island any minute, probably armed to the teeth, didn't cheer him any. He wanted the women gone by then.

"What if we don't have time to go get help?" Gina voiced his worst fear. "The exchange could be going down in hours. Can we reach Hariumat and have the teams get here that fast?"

Frustration burned through him. "I don't know." Had they gotten this far only to fail at the last second? Not if he had anything to say about it. He was determined to fight to the bitter end.

At the beginning of the mission he'd thought success was such a far shot, he didn't really worry about the endgame. And now here they were and everything could come down to a matter of minutes.

The trees thinned ahead of them a little, the soil turning rocky. They broke into a run, not slowing until they reached the bunker finally.

She yelled in through the door. "Anybody still here?"

No response came from inside.

He took in the untouched lock on the door. "How did you get out?"

"Through an air shaft. They're probably at the beach already. They might have seen your yacht."

He could see it from here, bobbing on the

surface of the water where he had anchored it a few hundred feet offshore. There was no sight of the ship Gina had talked about. Not yet. Then again, morning mist still hung over the ocean. In an hour, when the sun cleared that up, who knew what they would see out there?

They had to get the yacht away from here.

Gina turned onto the path that led to the beach. He caught sight of her arms and reached out to turn her toward him. He hadn't noticed until now how badly she was messed up—red welts running down her soft skin, dried blood sitting on top of some serious gouges.

"Are you okay?"

"Yeah." She shrugged it off and tugged him to go.

Instead of letting her, he pulled her closer, tight to him but careful not to squeeze her injuries. Her golden-brown eyes went wide, but she didn't protest.

Her hair was all messed up, her face smudged with dirt. Her clothes were filthy and torn. But her eyes flashed with determination. She was magnificent.

"I was worried about you," he said and kissed her, mindful that it very well could be the last time he was afforded that pleasure.

And as she relaxed in his arms, he realized something else. He knew with sudden clarity that she could have never been just an adventure, another light affair. And he regretted bitterly that most likely they would never find out what could have been.

He was a reasonable sort of man, not given to flights of fancy and wild optimism. He had a fair idea of what was waiting for him in the next couple of hours. He was willing to play his part to the end, but that didn't mean he didn't have regrets.

He leaned his forehead against hers, wanting to keep her like that forever, in his arms, safe. But she couldn't be safe if she stayed with him. He kissed her again, the way a man kissed a woman he realized he wanted more than anything, a woman he was about to lose.

Time. Never enough of that, was there? He tasted her, letting his passion pour into her, claiming her for his own, making sure he gave her something to remember him by.

Then he broke away. "I wish it could have been different. We'd better go, luv," he said.

GINA STUMBLED AFTER him toward the shore. Dizzy from the kiss, from the emotions in it. Wow. What was that about? And what was the tingling that coursed through her body, surrounding her heart with a ring of pleasure?

It was as if more than their bodies had touched with that kiss. She watched his broad shoulders as he made way through the undergrowth for her, holding back branches, kicking vines out of the way. The more she knew Cal Spencer, the more she liked him, the more she could imagine—

She couldn't think about this now.

She tried her best to focus on the path ahead and resolved to talk to him once they reached the neighboring island, the commando teams were sent off and they could finally relax.

They reached the end of the woods in half an hour. No sign of the others. A quick run down the beach revealed footprints in the sand. They led to the water.

"Cheeky Yanks, the lot of them. I think they commandeered the yacht," he said and smiled, but it had a bittersweet tinge.

She didn't have time to analyze it as she waded into the water next to him and threw herself into the choppy waves. When she looked up, she could see Anita on board, waving.

Had the others been waiting for them?

She glanced over at Cal. They were swimming head-to-head. The salty water stung her scrapes, and for a moment she considered just how smart it was to go into the water with arms that were bloodied. Were there sharks in these waters? None in the bay, according to Mark. She had asked before she'd gone out swimming on their first day here. But what about this side of the island?

She settled into a steady rhythm, focusing on nothing but the distance before her, keeping close to Cal. They reached the boat about the same time. Cal went first and helped her up.

"We have to go. Tsernyakov is coming." Gina got the most important thing out in between grabbing big gulps of air. "By air. The ship we saw is bringing the buyers, probably, to make the pickup."

Then Cal took over and gave them a quick heads-up on everything he knew. "You have to go. Now. I'm staying," he said when he was done.

What was he talking about? Gina spun to look at him as her heart took a slow, loud thump. "They'll kill you if they figure out you helped us." Didn't he get it?

"They won't." He looked determined. "You can drop me off at that crag." He pointed to a rocky outcropping on the beach to the west of them. "There might not be time for the commando team on standby to get here before the deal goes down. I have to go back and try something. I'll swim to shore and tell them I ran into pirates who dumped me overboard and took everything."

The wind was picking up, tossing the yacht. Gina grabbed on to the railing. "Will they buy it?" She hated the idea. "What if someone takes out the other chopper to find the yacht?" He couldn't see Tsernyakov's men letting this go so easily.

"Not right away. They won't have time to investigate right now. Tsernyakov is coming," he reminded them. "Everybody is running around like mad to prepare for him."

"Not to be a drag or anything, but none of us can drive a boat," Sam remarked.

Gina relaxed a little and sent her a thankful smile. Cal would have to come with them now.

He didn't look swayed. "You'll learn. I have to go back and create a distraction. I have to do something to slow down the handover. Look, I know I probably can't stop it, but if I could hold them back just for an hour—a half an hour even—it might make all the difference."

His eyes and jaw were hard-set and determined, and she realized he had thought this out, perhaps while he'd been on his way to save them. He had made his plans and nothing was going to deter him.

Her heart sank. She wished she had some good points she could use to talk him out of this madness, but she couldn't come up with anything at the moment. He was right about the situation. She hated that.

"Okay, so, new plan." She pulled herself straight and drew a deep breath. If Cal was going back, it was even more important that they got help as soon as possible. "How do we drive a boat?"

"If it runs on a computer, I can figure it out, probably." Carly moved toward the pilothouse.

"I'll show you the basics." Cal followed her and did just that, even digging out a user's manual. "You think you can handle it?" he asked after giving her some bare-bones instructions.

"We don't have any other choice, do we?" Carly asked, then said, "Don't worry about it. You do your part, we do ours."

"We are not altogether helpless," Anita said.

He grinned at them. "I noticed."

"We're not going that far," Carly put in with a good measure of self-confidence that went a long way toward settling Gina's nerves.

"Watch what I'm doing." He steered the boat and moved it toward the crag he'd indicated earlier, pointing to the displays and explaining how they helped with navigation.

"After you drop me off, you go a few hundred feet more on the same course to this point here." He jabbed the map with his index finger. "Then you turn the boat northwest at a forty-eight-degree angle. After that it's a straight line. You should see the island in about two hours if you keep your speed steady."

He handed the controls over to Carly, who didn't seem nervous about taking them. Then he moved back to grab the fire extinguisher fixed to the wall of the pilothouse. He used it to break a hole in one of the cabinets under the instrument panel.

"Here you go." He pulled out a couple of handguns, Russian-made Makarovs. "If you do run into pirates, use these and go for speed." Then he told them which restaurant to go to once they got to Hariumat, how to find the hidden phone, what number to call. He wanted to make sure his people were alerted as well as their own connection.

"What about the cyclone?" Gina asked. "You said it's coming from the west." The way they were going.

"Still too far out. Don't stray off course and get into its path and you'll be fine. You should be safely in harbor by the time it comes our way." He moved to the side of the boat. "Take care," he said to all of them, but his gaze rested on Gina.

"You, too," she said and wished he could have taken one of the guns. No use, of course. The water would render it unusable. "Stay safe."

He stood up there for a long second, wide shoulders outlined against the sky, hair flitting in the wind. Then he flashed one of those cocky grins of his and pushed away, diving into the water without looking back.

Carly waited until he was safely away from the yacht before starting up the engine again. She kept the yacht parallel to land, as Cal had instructed. Gina stayed where she was, following his progress as he swam to shore, ran across the sand and took off into the woods.

Then she began to think.

How on earth was he going to cause a big enough distraction all by himself?

Tsernyakov's goons outnumbered him twenty to one. He wasn't a trained professional in the first place; what was he going to do with his makeshift SIS training? The more she thought about it, the dimmer the situation seemed. He had to know that he didn't stand a chance. Why had he gone?

He was intelligent enough to realize—

And then it hit her that he did know. He was well aware that he'd gone back on a suicide mission. And he'd done it anyway, making sure first that they were all safe.

I wish it could have been different.

His words, which she'd barely registered in the aftermath of that kiss, made perfect sense now. Cal Spencer expected to die on the island, holding up the transaction until the commando teams got there.

She swallowed, her heart aching so badly she had to press a fist against her chest. She was law enforcement, dammit—or at least she had been. She had years of training and experience. If anyone stayed behind, it should have been her.

Maybe it wasn't too late.

"Stop the boat!" she yelled over the noise of the engine, turning toward Carly. "Stop the boat."

She did so immediately, looking at Gina wide-eyed and bewildered. "What's wrong?"

Anita was coming around. "What happened?"

"I'm going back." She took a deep breath. "I have to do this." She turned quickly and jumped without giving them a chance to try and talk her out of it.

She went under, kicked her way to the surface and gasped for air, could hear her friends shouting for her but ignored them. They would go. They knew how important it was to get the information to Brant and the commando team.

The current was stronger here than where she had swum to the yacht with Cal and coming head-on, trying to carry her back out to sea, making it harder to reach shore. She put her head down and gave it everything she had. She was not going to let Cal go into this alone, was not going to let him sacrifice himself, dammit. Who the hell did he think he was? Who elected him hero of the day?

She hung on to the anger to give her strength and because she couldn't allow the fear in—fear that she knew well from experience could paralyze a person. Anger was a better emotion right now; it gave her steam.

She was gasping for air by the time she reached shore. She stopped just long enough to catch her breath and squeeze some water out of her clothes. The shortest way to the bay would have been through the jungle, but could she manage that without getting turned around? This wasn't the time to take a risk. She moved into the cover of the trees and began walking parallel to the beach, rounding the cape.

She followed the yacht with her gaze as long as she could. "Good luck," she whispered as it disappeared from sight and wondered if they would ever see each other again.

The noise of a helicopter reached her, but she couldn't see anything from between the towering trees. She broke into a run, ignoring the vines that grabbed at her.

Tsernyakov was here.

She ran faster. She had to find Cal and let him know she'd come back. The two of them would have to come up with a plan.

She made it around the cape in an hour or so, could see the bay finally. She pulled a little deeper into the woods to make sure nobody spotted her. Another half hour brought her in line with the buildings. Where was Cal?

She watched and waited.

People were running around, taking care of

business. Where was Tsernyakov? Had the buyer's ship reached the other side of the island yet? How soon was the handover supposed to take place?

She had nothing but questions.

Where was Cal, dammit? What if Mark had figured out that he was lying and shot him on sight?

She continued walking, watching the activity on shore, the people who were coming and going from the bungalows and the main building. Then she caught a shadow moving at the edge of the woods about two hundred feet ahead.

She stilled for a second but could see nothing else, couldn't make out a human form among the trees. She picked her way forward carefully, not daring to pick up speed or make too much noise until she was close enough to make a positive ID. Then she began to run.

Cal whirled on her, his eyes going wide first with surprise, then with exasperation. "What are you doing here? What happened to the boat?"

"On its way." She walked up to him, breathing hard. She'd been pushing herself to get here on time.

He pulled her to him, tight to his chest, and enfolded her into his strong arms. And when she tilted her head to look into his eyes, he lowered his lips to hers and kissed her. And for those few seconds everything melted away.

"Where were you going?" she asked after they moved apart.

"To the helipad to disable the choppers. I want to make sure nobody is leaving before the teams get here. I want to see what I can do about the terrorists' boat, too."

He moved forward and she fell in step next to him. He didn't admonish her or try to send her back to safety, which she appreciated.

"What did Mark say?"

"Haven't seen him yet. By the time I got here I didn't have time for explanations. I was going to blow up the utility building or something to cause confusion. But I realized that if I did that now, my cousin would just get back on his chopper and get away."

"So you figured you would trap everyone on the island until help gets here?"

"That's the plan. Your friends have the yacht. I swam up to the motorboats and took care of those already. I'll decommission the choppers, then go to the bunkers. That's where the virus is. Everyone will have to go there at some point."

"You can't blow that up."

"Right. The buyers will come to shore in a boat from their ship. All we need to do is to take that boat out."

"So basically we will be stuck on the island

with a bunch of terrorists when U.S. and U.K. commandos open fire and start World War III?"

His face turned somber. "That about sums it up. You should have stayed on the yacht." A world of regret swam in his eyes.

"And leave you to have all the fun?"

He mumbled something about the meddling nature of American women but reached for her arm and ran a hand over it gently, skirting her injuries. "The sea cleaned it up fairly well."

"Remind me not to swim again with open wounds," she said.

They were nearing the stables and the corral, and he turned that way instead of up the hill toward the helipad.

"What are we doing here?"

"Going on foot would be hopelessly slow. We need horses."

"I thought you were scared of them."

He glared. "I didn't say scared. I just wouldn't go on horseback given another choice."

A mite touchy, are we? She turned so he wouldn't see her grinning. The area was deserted. Everybody was down by the bay.

They sneaked by the horses in the corral and went straight to the stables, where they would be shielded from view. There were more animals in here, in their stalls. Cal picked two and began saddling them.

"How do you know how to do that?" she asked as she watched him strap more leather accessories on the animal than a South Street dominatrix wore on her best day.

"I was made to do it as a child. Very traumatic, actually," he said, but a smile played at the corner of his lips.

"Obviously." She rolled her eyes. Then swallowed when he handed her the reins of the smaller horse.

She grabbed on. The animal didn't blink an eye. So far, so good.

"The idea is to get them into the jungle without anyone spotting us," he said.

She tugged at the reins. The horse followed. "Piece of cake." The horse stopped at the next bale of hay and began to eat. She yanked on the rein without success. The animal would not budge, would not even lift his head. Great. Couldn't even get the damn thing out of the barn. "Now what?"

"Maybe you can tempt her with that piece of cake." His upper lip twitched.

"Very funny." But it gave her an idea. She grabbed a fistful of hay, then wagged it in front of the horse. The animal lifted its head. "There you go. Come on."

She shot Cal a triumphant look when the monstrous thing followed.

"Brilliant," he said and looked outside. "All clear."

The first clump of trees was no more than thirty feet away. They reached it without incident.

"Should we get on?" She swallowed the lump in her throat. The saddle looked way too high. She could certainly understand Cal's reluctance about all this.

"Better get farther in. In case the horses rear or whatever. I'd rather be completely out of sight."

"Rear?"

"Not that I think that would happen. Definitely not," he said, but he did look nervous around the edges.

They reached the thicker part of the woods.

"Always get on from the left," he said and put his foot in the stirrup to demonstrate. "See? Nothing to it." He sat ramrod straight in the saddle. "Now you try."

She heaved, slid back, heaved again and made it this time. The horse swayed under her. "Do they always move this much?"

"From what I recall, unfortunately, yes." His horse moved forward.

"How do you make them go?"

"With your heel. Lean forward, too, a little. Squeeze your thighs. You stop them by pulling up on the reins and leaning back in the saddle."

"Anything else I should know?"

"Keep the rein taut. Not loose, not too tight. Tightening the left will make her go that way. Tightening the right—"

"Okay. I get it." She touched her heels to the horse's side and squeezed her thighs.

Nothing happened. "By the time I figure out how this works… Don't you think we could have gotten there faster on foot?"

"Sadly, no. Squeeze harder. Click with your tongue."

She did. The horse began to move.

"Faster," he said.

She squeezed even harder and clicked again. The horse broke into a trot. She held on for dear life, developing a whole new respect for the mounted police.

"You okay?" she asked him, although he looked fine to her, sitting on the horse securely. Kind of sexy, actually.

"I have bigger things to worry about." He held her gaze for a moment. "You shouldn't have come back."

"Get over it. It's good to have someone to watch your back when you're going into something dangerous."

"This goes beyond dangerous, luv. I would have preferred knowing you're safe."

"I have no intention of coming to harm. And if you even think about some noble English crap like sacrificing yourself, I'm going to be seriously ticked."

His lips stretched into a grin. "I'll keep that in mind."

The sound of a motor came from the bay. She turned back in the saddle and caught a glimpse of a pickup truck. Two guys in camouflage Army fatigues got out, then a tall, dark-haired man in a suit. He carried himself like royalty.

She looked back to where she was going, not daring to take her eyes off the animal for too long.

"My cousin," Cal said, his voice tight.

She stole a quick glance again. "I pictured him different."

"Expected fangs and horns?"

"Just more…" What? "Menacing-looking." Sounded stupid now that she said it out loud.

"Trust me, he's bloody scary on the inside."

She stole another peek. "Couldn't we take the pickup?"

"You want to go back for it?"

She looked at the two dozen armed men swarming on the beach. "Horses are fine," she said.

Chapter Nine

She had to admit the horses did come in handy. They were at the choppers in thirty minutes. On foot it would have taken them close to two hours.

Cal stopped his horse before they got to the clearing and slid out of the saddle.

She did the same. "Better tie them up."

He took the reins from her and tied both horses to a low-swung branch of a flowering hibiscus. They immediately began nibbling on the leaves.

Cal stole forward.

She followed.

The clearing seemed deserted. Two helicopters sat on a flat area where vegetation and rocks had been removed and the ground was packed hard and relatively even.

"You know anything about these?" she asked belatedly.

"I flew a couple of times when I was doing

business with a megacompany. They sent the corporate chopper for me. Very plush."

He *flew* in a chopper? That was the extent of his knowledge?

"We're doomed," she said before she could stop herself.

He just flashed that cocky grin. "How hard can it be? We're practically superspies."

She raised her eyebrows. "Strong emphasis on *practically*."

"You and I can do anything together," he said, holding her gaze.

Warmth spread through her suddenly. She swallowed. "Damn right," she said before she could melt into a puddle at his feet. "Let's get to it."

But he went still and put a hand out to hold her back, staring at the larger chopper. His body language transmitted *imminent danger*.

She responded by drawing back and scanning the clearing. "What is it?" she asked, keeping her voice to a whisper.

"We've got company."

She stared harder and did spot a dark shape in the chopper, somebody sitting in the back. Whoever it was didn't move. Why not? He had to have seen them. They were out in the open.

"Dead?" She had no trouble picturing Tsernyakov dealing harshly with insubordination.

"I think he's sleeping." Cal skirted toward the smaller chopper, moving in a crouch, keeping out of the line of vision of the man in the other one.

She followed him, observing the same precautions. When he got to the door, he opened it without a sound. "Get in."

She'd never been in a helicopter before. Looked smaller on the inside than she'd thought. She took the front passenger seat and glanced around. A slew of gauges took up most of the space in front of the pilot. The window came down lower than in a car.

Cal was rummaging through the back and came up with a toolbox and took out a sizable screwdriver. He popped off the instrument panel. "Hold this."

"Are you sure you haven't done this before? You look like you know what you're doing," she said.

"Now that I'm seeing it up close, it's not much different from a car. We are not trying to fix it. We want to break the thing. That's always the easier part, isn't it? People break stuff they know nothing about all the time."

His calm logic reassured her, and she watched with fascination as he switched to a smaller screwdriver and loosened a number of bolts and took them out, shoved them into his pocket. He wiggled out a small piece of metal, then another, then looked at his handiwork with a good measure of self-satisfaction.

He looked very adventurous and handsome and

capable. But it wasn't just his looks she was attracted to. Although she hated to admit that, because it begged the question: what was she going to do about her wayward feelings?

He turned and grinned at her, the combination of those lips and his sparkling green-blue eyes enough to steal her breath away. "That should do."

With some effort, she put everything else but the mission from her mind. "That's it?"

"Engineering is an efficient science. I don't think there are any spare parts in there that don't do anything."

Made sense. Still, she wished they had a gun so they could put some bullets into that instrument panel. She was familiar with guns. When in doubt, people tended to resort to what they knew. But they didn't have a firearm, so she had to trust Cal's mechanical skills.

He went to work on some wires and she watched him intermittently, searching around her seat with her free hand…and hit pay dirt. She pulled a SIG Sauer from under the backseat. "Look." She half expected him to ask for it and was prepared to make an argument.

But all he said was, "Brilliant. You keep it. You have more experience with guns."

The acknowledgment felt good. "Need help?" She pointed it at the top row of instruments.

"I'd rather not make noise if we can do this quietly." He didn't take his eyes off what he was doing.

"What about the other chopper?"

"Too risky."

"There are two of us."

"Let's keep it that way," he said. "If the guy gets off a single shot, it'll be heard in the bay."

"Then we ride to the other side of the island?"

He made a face as he looked toward the horses, but he said, "You bet."

His reluctance around horses messed with her head. He was all capable and smooth and suave and all that, a mix of masculinity and European elegance. She found that much perfection intimidating. The fact that he had a chink in his armor made him more lovable. *Likable*. Likable was what she'd meant.

She slipped out of the chopper, annoyed at her train of thought, and strode toward the jungle. Maybe if she was fast enough, she could outrun all this weirdness she was beginning to feel when she was around the man.

THE SHIP WAS VISIBLE now, anchored offshore. Cal watched the beach from the cover of the trees. No boats anywhere, no sign that any of the terrorists had come to shore yet.

"They probably have a time set for the meeting when they'll come in for the handover." Gina kept an eye on the ship.

"Or Joseph will take the virus to them." He thought about that for a second. "Not likely, though, is it? He would want the exchange to happen on his own turf to give him the strategic advantage in case his business partners are up to no good."

"What if *he* is up to no good?" Gina looked at him. She looked a little scruffy, her hair messed up from the swim, her face smudged. Scruffy and hot, like some comic-book heroine preparing for the showdown fight.

"What if he takes the money but won't deliver the goods?" she asked.

"An out-and-out fight where Joseph's men and the terrorists take each other out? A nice fantasy but probably too much to hope for. He always delivers. That's why he has the reputation he does. That's why he's the biggest."

They waited silently for a few minutes. Nothing happened. There was no movement near the ship that they could see from this distance. The winds were much worse now than a few hours earlier, and for a second he thought about the other women, how they were handling the rough seas. The sky was darkening toward the west.

"Let's check out what's going on at the bunker,"

Gina recommended, eyeing the swirling clouds. "Maybe Tsernyakov's men are already there. Maybe we can raise some mayhem, slow them down."

He thought about that for a second. They did have a gun and the element of surprise on their side. If they could get their hands on the virus and hide it until the commando teams got here... It would be a miracle. But the bunker in question was just a few hundred yards from where they were, and there seemed to be nothing to do here. He was too pumped up on adrenaline to sit around and stare at the sea. He turned and walked back into the jungle.

"Wonder how far Anita and the others are from Hariumat." Gina walked beside him.

He glanced at his watch. "They should be there soon." But would it be soon enough? The wind was picking up, shaking the canopy above them, dislodging leaves and small branches.

Although the incoming storm covered any noise they made, they moved slowly, going as carefully as possible, knowing that they might not find the bunker deserted this time. They didn't want to run into Joseph's men. Their caution paid off. They saw the enemy before the enemy saw them. They crawled in the cover of the bushes to get close enough to hear.

"I'm starving," someone said in Russian. "How long do we have to sit here?"

"Until the boss says we can go," another responded.

Gina flashed him a questioning look, probably wanting to know what the men were talking about. He'd learned Russian from his mother.

He shook his head and made a diminishing gesture with his hand. "Nothing," he mouthed. Nothing important.

How many were they? He stole forward another couple of feet, keeping under the cover of some big-leafed evergreen. Four men sat around the opening of the bunker, each armed to the teeth. He didn't recognize any from the island. They must have come with the chopper. The front door was open. Were there more inside?

"Plenty of food and water in there," one of the men said.

His buddy made a face. "Not worth getting any bones broken over. We're not supposed to touch nothing."

Cal pulled back to Gina to a point where he could still hear the men but didn't have to worry about them getting lucky and catching a glimpse of him.

"What now?" Gina mouthed.

"We wait." Making a move without knowing

how many people they were up against was too risky. As long as they kept their eye on the virus they always had a chance to mess up the handover.

A walkie-talkie crackled to life by the bunker a few minutes later. Too much static and wind to hear what was said from this distance. This time when he sneaked closer, Gina followed.

The men were nowhere to be seen.

They kept low and waited. Then a guy appeared, alert and with AK-47 in hand, ready for action. Two others came behind carrying a stainless steel cooler. After them walked another one, also well armed, Sergey bringing up the rear. He must have been in the bunker earlier.

Cal exchanged a look with Gina. They were outnumbered five to two. He doubted anyone would stay behind at the bunker. No sense in guarding the place now that it was empty. Five well-armed men against the two of them and their sole weapon. But the odds didn't matter much when they didn't have a choice. There were no decisions to be made. They had to try something. The men were headed for the shore.

The handover was going down. Now. By the time the commando team got here, the virus would be long gone. It was up to Gina and him.

They followed close by, halted when Sergey stopped to light a smoke. The path they followed was choked with vegetation and vines hanging from the trees above. In seconds Sergey's buddies passed out of sight.

Gina signaled toward him. Cal nodded.

The next second she rushed the man from behind, gun to the back of his head.

Sergey spun.

Gina had her index finger across her lips in a gesture to remain silent, although, as much noise as the trees were making, bending in the wind, Sergey would have had to be pretty loud to be heard. They just had to make sure he didn't get a chance to discharge his gun.

Cal kept in the bushes and got behind him while he was distracted, hit him hard in the back of the head with a fallen branch. It only stunned him, didn't knock him out. Still, he hesitated for long enough for Gina to grab the AK-47 from him. She smacked him with the butt of the rifle and watched with satisfaction as the man crumpled to the forest floor before handing Cal the weapon.

"Good work." He swung the AK-47 across his shoulder and grabbed the man under the armpits.

Gina picked up his feet, and together they dragged him off the path. When he was tied to a tree with his own belt, Gina tried to rip a piece of the guy's shirt for a gag. The material was heavy enough not to give.

She groaned with frustration, then a wicked smile spread on her face as she tugged Sergey's boots off first, then his socks, then stuck the latter in his mouth.

"I hope you never get mad at me for anything." Cal grimaced.

"You should try your best to stay on my good side." She grinned and took off after the others on the path.

The trees soon gave way to sand and that was as far as they could follow. They couldn't come out into the open, but they were close enough to observe the beach. A boat was coming to shore.

The men ahead just noticed that Sergey was missing. They looked back a couple of times and shouted his name. Then one remarked that he was probably taking a leak.

"Do you think they'll come back to look for him?" Gina asked, getting the gist of what was going on even without knowing the language.

"Unlikely." He watched as a pickup came around the cape, riding on the sand with two men in the cab.

"Mark," he told Gina. "The other one is Joseph."

The pickup stopped.

The buyers ran the motorboat to shore and were jumping into the shallow water.

Then Joseph and Mark got out, as well, and everyone began to move toward some spot in the middle. The whole picture was surreal, resembling a harmless meeting of bootleggers instead of a handover between ruthless criminals who were about to alter history and send countless innocent people to death.

"Time to cut off the avenue of retreat," he said, using an expression he'd learned during his SIS training, slipping the rifle from his shoulder. "Be careful."

He held her gaze for a moment, wishing they could have met under different circumstances. He leaned forward for a kiss while inside he raged against the unfairness of life. She clung to him. If he hadn't already known how bad the situation was, this would have clued him in. Gina didn't cling. She was tough as anything. He pulled away with a world of regrets choking him up.

"We can't make a mistake." He cupped her face with his free hand. "As soon as we fire the first shot they'll know where we are."

Steely determination hardened her face. "I guess we just have to make sure we don't miss. I take the boat, you take the pickup."

The boat was the more difficult mark, with the waves in constant motion behind it. She didn't seem intimidated by the task. She was the hottest woman he'd ever met, all fire and rock-solid.

"One, two, three," he said, and they aimed for the gas tanks.

The boat and the vehicle went up in simultaneous explosions.

Confusion ruled on the shore, everyone running for the cover of the trees, running toward them, spraying the tree line with bullets in front of them as they neared.

"Go, go, go." He covered Gina as they ran ahead on the path. They couldn't hold off eleven armed men. They had to get someplace where they had decent cover and a strategic advantage.

He ran toward the closest bunker, followed by Gina, but after a few minutes realized that the men weren't following them. Where in bloody hell had they gone?

"They are going for the chopper," Gina said, catching on to what was happening at the same time he did.

The handover was a bust. Neither party trusted the other enough to be sure that they hadn't been set up. Everyone was clamoring to get out of here.

He and Gina had an advantage now, even if it was an advantage of mere seconds. Cal took off after them, praying they wouldn't be too late.

"There are eleven of them and only one working chopper." Gina ran close behind.

Hope bubbled up through the rush of adrenaline. If they fought amongst themselves, it would give Gina and him time to catch up with the bastards. They still had the cooler. Under no circumstances could the virus leave the island.

When they reached the clearing, both helicopters were chock-full of men, the rotors going already. Two of the terrorists were trying to get the cooler into the smaller chopper.

Both Gina and he aimed at the men in the bigger one, not wanting to hit the virus by accident. The chopper lifted off temporarily, then touched back down with a hideous noise. A moment passed while the pilot tried again, all the while the others shooting through the open doors.

Then it became obvious that the bird wasn't taking off anytime soon and people began pouring out of the helicopter. A few went for the other one; others ran for the woods, wary of getting caught between the bullets Gina and Cal were squeezing off and those coming from the other chopper.

The cooler was dragged in just as Gina picked off one of the men trying to get in after it, while Cal picked off the other. The chopper was lifting off. Other than the pilot, there were three men inside. They kept shooting in Cal and Gina's direction and, for the most, kept them flattened behind the trees.

It wasn't going to work this way. He had to give up his cover in order to do what he had to do.

"Cover me." Cal rushed forward without giving her a chance to protest, without giving himself a chance to think, really. The time for sheer gut reaction was here; nothing but that and a serious dose of luck could save them now.

He ran while Gina did her best, hitting the chopper with her few remaining bullets. She couldn't have too many left.

The chopper was six feet off the ground and rising.

He dived forward and jumped, grabbed on to the skid at the last minute but didn't have as much as a split second to marvel that he'd actually made it. Instead of staying covered, Gina was running after him.

"Get back!" He'd meant to do whatever it took to crash that chopper into the ocean. He didn't want her to be on it.

GINA JUMPED FOR THE other skid, opposite Cal, without thinking, acting on sheer adrenaline in the heat of the moment, ignoring the fierce look he was giving her. She silently thanked her mother for all those gymnastics lessons. All that good balance and hand-eye coordination was about to come in handy.

The helicopter pulled up sharply and all of a sudden there was considerable distance between her and the ground, growing by the second. *Omigod, omigod.* Reality hit her. This wasn't the uneven bars. She was dangling from a chopper in midair. And even if she pulled off some wild acrobatics, she was unarmed. She'd tossed the SIG when it'd run out of bullets. Was it too late to jump? She looked down and swallowed the lump in her throat. Definitely too late.

She glanced over at Cal, who was still glaring at her. He was unarmed, as well, having had to let go of the rifle to jump after the chopper.

"Up?" he asked—or she thought he did. The rotors were deafeningly loud.

He gestured upward with his head and extended one hand to her. Was she supposed to go over there?

Not in a million years. She shook her head, holding on for dear life. She didn't mind the acrobatics, but she hated heights. Unfortunately her arms were killing her already. Hanging from a moving object required a hell of a lot of strength. If she didn't get in, she would fall in minutes, especially with the way the chopper was jerking around in the high winds that were getting stronger now by the second.

Could this even be done in real life? The whole

scenario was unreal, something out of a movie. But if the stunt doubles could do it...

She took a deep breath and let go with one hand, reached for his. Their fingertips touched first. She leaned out more until her hand was clamped over his wrist and his around hers.

Rain started suddenly, without warning, and pelted them from above. What else could go wrong? She gritted her teeth, determined not to be done in either by nature or by conscienceless bastard terrorists.

Cal held her gaze and nodded. And she put her life into his hands, literally, taking a deep breath and pitching forward.

Her heart stopped for that moment when she hung in midair. She kicked her feet on instinct, then stopped herself, realizing she was making matters worse. Then her free hand closed around the metal bar and she pulled herself up, gaining purchase with both hands after a second.

She didn't have a chance to catch her breath, had to grip tighter as the helicopter lurched from the sudden shift of weight. She held her breath while the pilot steadied the chopper again, struggling against the wind.

She needed a moment of respite before they began climbing for the door. She didn't get it. The barrel of a rifle appeared in her line of view.

"Watch out!" Gina warned.

This was it. They were going to die.

She looked into Cal's eyes, wanting him to be the last thing she saw instead of the flare out of the end of the barrel.

But when the bullets came, they missed them by a wide margin. The shooter couldn't see them; he was squeezing the trigger blind.

Cal didn't give him a chance to get into a better position. He grabbed the barrel and heaved. A dark mass flew by them with a drawn-out scream. She didn't have it in her to look after the man. They were still over the island. He wasn't going to have a soft landing.

"Three more to go," Cal shouted over the noise that seemed to pulsate in her brain.

He reached up, hooked his leg, then in a few moments disappeared from sight. Gunshots exploded above. The chopper lurched again, leaving her dangling precariously, threatening to send her after the man she'd just seen fall to his death. Not a happy thought. She had to get up there.

Don't look down. Don't look down. Swing, catch, pull.

She had to climb over one dead body to get in, to get to the hand-to-hand combat Cal was fighting. The pilot was going for his weapon.

Gina grabbed the dead man's handgun and put it to the pilot's head, ignored the hate on his face and the savage swearing and threats she couldn't understand.

"Set the chopper down," Gina shouted at the man at the end of the barrel.

Where was Tsernyakov? She looked around bewildered. He hadn't been in the other chopper, either. The crafty bastard probably had a whole list of backup plans and hadn't fancied getting on a chopper with his terrorist business partners who might blame him for the screwup, nor with a cooler full of virus phials.

She kept one eye on the pilot and one on Cal and the other guy fighting in the back. The cooler was strapped down not far from them. At one point the terrorist hurled Cal against it, and she held her breath until Cal fought him off, with inherent elegance, and they moved away. There was nothing she could do to help him. She had to stay where she was to control the pilot. "Set it down."

"Or what? You shoot me?" the man shouted back in broken English. "Who is going to fly it?"

Cal finally got in a solid punch. The man he fought teetered back and crumpled.

"I will," she bluffed straight-faced.

The man put his hands in the air and leaned back. "Go ahead."

She held his gaze. With each passing second his grin got wider. Slowly he took control of the levers again.

"Land. Now." Cal had come up. He reached into his pocket, then extended his hand in front of the pilot's face. The parts he'd taken out of the other chopper lay in his palm. The winds tossed the chopper now as if it weighed no more than a seagull. "Do it before we crash."

The pilot's gaze flew to the dashboard, then back to the nuts and bolts. He swore in Russian again. Then he adjusted a few things and the helicopter began to descend.

She held her breath the entire time, gripping the gun hard enough to get a cramp in her wrist, not daring to move it, worried that the pilot might still have some trick up his sleeve.

But just this once, in the middle of their worst-case scenario, their luck finally held and he didn't make any sudden moves.

They barely touched down before she turned the handgun around and slammed the butt into the back of the man's head. Then she shot up the dashboard for good measure. Nobody else was going to take this chopper anywhere.

Cal was grinning at her, his masculine lips stretched from ear to ear.

"What are you so happy about?"

"You're really sexy when you take care of business, you know?" He jumped to the ground and she followed.

Sexy had been the last thing on her mind. Served to show that all that research stating what men thought about an average of every seven seconds was exactly right on the money.

She would have mentioned it to him but was cut off when hell broke loose somewhere around the bay. Three explosions followed each other in quick succession, the sound of other helicopters filling the air.

Did Tsernyakov get back to the bay already? Was he doing all this? He must have had a backup plan. She hoped against hope that the choppers had been sent by Brant, but it seemed too soon for that. Hariumat wasn't that close.

"The cooler. Quick." Cal reached back and was unfastening the restraints already. "Even if it's our backup, they might decide to take out these choppers from the air, not knowing what's inside. It would be better for all involved if we didn't let the virus get airborne."

She helped him lift the heavy cooler to the ground. The choppers were nearly on top of them.

"Go, go, go." Cal ran toward the woods.

She followed, holding up the other end. They just made it into cover when the two Apache helicopters came into view. The choppers on the ground were history in a few seconds.

"They're here." Cal visibly relaxed.

"Thank God." But she wasn't sure that they were out of the woods just yet. "We'd better get rid of this." She nodded toward the cooler, not altogether comfortable to be this close to a deadly virus.

In the confusion of the battle, it would be too easy to meet up with one of the enemy or even some gung-ho commando soldier who thought to shoot first and ask questions later. She didn't want to walk out onto the beach with the cooler in her hands.

"By the tower?" Cal asked.

A spot easily found again and not too far from here. "Perfect."

They took off running in that direction, going as fast as the uneven ground and the heavy case allowed. She could hear the choppers circling overhead but couldn't see them through the thick canopy. They reached the tower without trouble. When the cooler was hidden in the kudzu at the base of it, they started back.

"Backup got here faster than I thought," Cal remarked as they moved forward at a rapid speed, keeping an eye and ear out for soldiers and/or terrorists moving through the woods. The wind snatched some of his words, but she could make out enough to understand.

"That's my team." She grinned, grateful to Anita, Carly and Sam.

The whole nightmare was almost over. They'd done it, accomplished the impossible. And if they could do this, then wasn't it possible that they might be able to start new lives, as well? Despite the danger they were still in, hope coursed through her body, filling her with more optimism than she had felt in a long time.

Then Cal slowed, lifting his hand in a sign of warning. The next second, a man in a dark suit stepped from behind a clump of bushes—an expensive suit, although now heavily soiled. He held a gun but didn't point it at them.

"I wouldn't go that way." He nodded toward the direction he'd come from. "The bay is a mess."

"Good to see you in one piece, Joseph. Anyone make it with you?" Cal kept up the charade. "What in hell is going on?"

She stared. Joseph Tsernyakov, one of the most dangerous and evil men in the world, was standing not ten feet from her. She and the team had worked for so long that to get near him now felt surreal.

He looked so…ordinary. Good-looking, too, although she could see no family resemblance between the cousins. Maybe Cal was right and she had expected horns. She kept quiet, trying to melt into the background, letting Cal run the show.

"Some people are making a nuisance of themselves." Tsernyakov looked her over, raising his gun slightly.

Her heartbeat slowed as underlying tension filled the air.

Cal moved between them. His hand inched toward the gun at his back.

She willed the men not to make a move. They were all standing within a few feet of each other. No way to miss. The chances of who would end up dead on the ground were about even.

"Your friend?" Tsernyakov drew up an eyebrow as he lowered the gun casually, as if he'd never meant any harm at all. "We'll make the introductions later. Let's get to the choppers." He was walking that way already.

Gina shot Cal a questioning look, her pulse slowly returning to normal. He shook his head slightly.

"Good idea," he told Tsernyakov and fell in step behind him.

Tsernyakov waited, however, until they were in line with him, as if he didn't want them at his back.

Gina kept up with the men. Her handgun was tucked into the waistband of her shorts, behind her back, as was Cal's into his. Tsernyakov had his weapon in his hand. A pretty lousy setup.

He clearly didn't trust them. But then why was he taking them with him?

Insurance? If something went wrong, he could hold them as hostages.

Movement in the woods caught her eye. She didn't dare fully look that way. She didn't want to draw Tsernyakov's attention to it.

Chapter Ten

"Have you seen anyone else?" Tsernyakov asked.

The wind was howling now, bending trees, the rain soaking them to the skin.

"No. But we heard some choppers above," Cal said, giving Gina a look she couldn't understand.

What was he trying to tell her?

"What were you doing in the woods?" Tsernyakov kept grilling him. Then he looked at Gina and flashed a half grin. "Never mind."

If Cal meant to make a move now, what was he waiting for? Gina walked with them, expecting some sort of a clear signal that the time was now, but it never came. Then they finally reached the clearing and stopped to listen and watch for danger before they stepped out.

It was clear at first glance that both choppers were completely destroyed. Tsernyakov swore. Not as cool and unaffected as he appeared to be, was he?

"What do we do now?" Cal asked and moved into position so that, whatever happened, he would cover Gina with his body.

She made a point of moving away, trudging in mud that was deeper in the open area. She wanted a clear line of vision to Tsernyakov so she could shoot unencumbered when the time came.

"I have a boat hidden." Tsernyakov was cutting through the clearing already. "In case of emergency."

"In this weather?" Gina asked.

"I already called in a ship to pick me up." Movement behind the trees in their path cut him off.

The next second, a dozen camouflaged soldiers stepped from behind the trees and surrounded them, crowding them into the middle.

The three of them stood back-to-back. She still wasn't too happy with the setup. "Don't shoot," she yelled to no one in particular. The commando knew there were undercover operatives on the island.

"We can take them," Joseph said and aimed.

But Cal turned and pointed his gun at him instead. "No, we can't."

Gina followed Cal's example.

Surprise flashed through the man's eyes, then understanding, then fury. "How can you betray your family?" He spat at Cal but missed.

Cal didn't even flinch. "How can you betray humanity?"

The soldiers moved closer.

Tsernyakov pulled up his gun and aimed at his own head. Both of them lurched forward, but Cal was faster. He knocked the man's arm up, and the bullet went wide.

Tsernyakov didn't seem upset. She realized too late that the move had been just a feint. With attention diverted from his left hand for a split second, Tsernyakov grabbed her by the arm and spun her in front of him, shoving the barrel of his gun hard against her temple. "Back off."

Everything slowed for a second. Blood rushed through her ears so loud she couldn't hear what people were saying, although she could see their lips move. Then it all returned to normal just as suddenly, and she was alert and poised to fight, her training and experience on the force returning.

Everybody was shouting at once. "Drop your weapon! Drop your weapon!"

She could make out Brant's voice over the din. "Hold your fire!"

Where was he? She hadn't seen him before.

Tsernyakov would shoot if he didn't get what he wanted. He had nothing to lose. She needed to reassure him by complying. She relaxed her fingers and let her gun slide to the ground, cursing through clenched teeth. How could she have been so stupid and let him get hold of her?

"I want a chopper now," Tsernyakov said calmly, full of self-assurance, a man expecting his orders to be filled.

"Let her go." Cal put his hands in the air. "Take me. I'm bigger. I'll cover more of you."

"If I didn't think taking the gun off your little whore was a bad idea, you'd be dead by now," Tsernyakov responded. "Stay where you are. I don't want to see as much as a muscle twitch."

"Okay, okay." Brant made his way forward among the men of his commando team. "There isn't enough room for another chopper to land here. How about we put one down for you on the beach?"

Tsernyakov thought for a second. "On the south beach. And I want the whole beach cleared. I don't want to see a single boat on the water."

"Fine. Nothing but the chopper and the pilot." Brant sounded reassuring.

"No pilot."

He could fly? She wasn't overly surprised, actually. The man was notorious for mistrusting everyone. Made sense that he was prepared for every eventuality.

Would he take her with him?

Probably.

Then what?

Toss her into the ocean when they were far enough away?

"It might take a while to get one here in this weather." Law was playing for time.

Tsernyakov required but a split second to come up with the response. "You already have the Apaches here."

He could fly an Apache? Her future was looking dimmer by the minute. She shivered in the rain despite the fact that it wasn't that cold. Small branches dropped now and then from above, twisted off by the wind that wrestled with the treetops.

Tsernyakov held her by her midriff with his left hand, pointing the gun with his right. She glanced at her own weapon not three feet from where she stood in the mud. She had one chance to make a move. If she didn't succeed…

To hell with that. She looked into Cal's eyes. What she saw there was worth living for. She had no intention of failing.

Don't do it. Don't do it. Cal transmitted his silent message, but Gina looked determined to make some move. His heart had stopped beating when Joseph had grabbed her but now lurched into a sprint. All the double-oh stuff had been fun and games, but having Gina in danger— Fury burned through his veins.

He watched with horror as she fell forward with her full weight, pulling Joseph off balance. A shot rang out and went wide as the man came down on top of her. She lifted her head and smashed it into his nose with full force. Her other hand was going for her gun. Joseph pulled up his weapon to aim. All this happened in a brief moment, all at the same time. Then Cal jumped on top of his cousin, grabbing for his hand.

They were rushed the next second and disarmed in the blink of an eye.

Brant Law was there, extricating Gina from the bottom of the pile. "Undercover agent. She's with me," he said as a dozen guns pointed at them.

She reached over for Cal. "Undercover agent. He's with me," she said, repeating the agent's statement.

He liked the sound of that last sentence in particular.

Law was rolling his eyes, but a smile played on his lips, relief clearly evident on his face. "Capture by sandwich? Amateurs."

His men were hauling Tsernyakov aside.

"And where would the virus be?"

Gina told him in detail. He sent two men to retrieve the cooler, then turned to Cal. "Nice work here. There are a couple of British bad boys down the beach looking for you, Mr. Spencer."

He wished they'd been here and saved him from shaving ten years off his life by watching Gina in his cousin's clutches. "Glad you made it here," Cal told Law, then turned to Gina. "Are you all right?"

Brant was speaking at the same time. "You okay?" He was handing her a pair of handcuffs. "I thought you might want to do the honors."

She hesitated only for a second before taking them, brushing mud and wet leaf bits off her legs. "How are the others?"

Brant shook his head. "Wouldn't be left behind for anything. Why didn't that surprise me? You have a tight team."

"I've got good friends." It sounded as if there was a lump in her throat. "How did they get to you so fast? We didn't expect you for a while."

"We kept the island under surveillance from the air. Once we saw them go out on the boat, we sent in our men to meet them halfway."

The soldiers were holding Joseph. Gina marched right up to him and slapped the cuffs on. He drew his head back, and Cal realized he was planning on spitting on her.

"It's going to be hard wiping your broken nose with a broken arm," she said without flinching, in a voice any Wild West gunslinger would have been proud of.

Joseph swallowed. Then he let loose a nasty diatribe. Gina just looked at him and stuck her chin out. For a moment Cal thought she might do more. Her hands were fisting at her sides.

"You're not worth it," she said instead and turned away from the man.

Even as she walked, bent against the wind, Cal could detect a small spring in her step, a different look on her face, and realized just what Brant Law had given her back by handing her the cuffs. He reached a hand toward the man.

Brant accepted the handshake. "I know the situation you were put in. Thank you for what you've done."

And as they led Joseph away, Cal knew without a doubt that Gina had been right. Loyalty *was* a tricky thing. He had made the right decision. He had made a decision for justice and for the future, a future he hoped to share with the woman next to him.

How on earth was he going to convince her of that when she was the most independent, self-sufficient person he had ever met?

Joseph called out a few more obscenities to him and Gina. Cal stepped between them to block her from him. "Want me to shut him up?"

"Actually, he's taking his capture better than I thought he would," she said.

"He doesn't believe for a moment that the law could hold him. He probably thinks his connections will have him out by tonight." Cal looked after him, at the face distorted with hate. "He can't hurt us. He can't hurt anyone anymore."

"I promise you that," Brant agreed. "He has no idea how much we have on him. He will never see the outside of a prison again. Why don't you two go down to the bay? It's secured. There are teams going through the woods to pick up any stray targets. I'll send a man with you to make sure you don't run into trouble."

"Keep your men. You need them here. Others might come, trying to get away from the island, not knowing the choppers have been demolished," Cal said. "We can handle trouble." He wanted a few moments alone with Gina.

Brant looked at Tsernyakov, then at them. "I suppose you can."

GINA HURRIED THROUGH the jungle, eager to see the others and make sure they were all right, to thank them for bringing reinforcement.

"Mind stopping for a second?" Cal reached for her arm.

She stopped and turned.

"So…I've been thinking…" he said.

"When did you have the time?" Her mind was still reeling from everything that had happened.

"We are leaving the island today." His face was somber. He was still holding on to her arm.

She stared at him for a moment. They would leave today. Which meant he would go back to London, to his old life, while she would return to the U.S. to start her life over. The distance seemed real and insurmountable all of a sudden.

How soon would they have to part? Maybe as soon as they reached the bay. She wasn't ready for that.

She lifted her arms to his, as if the small gesture could somehow anchor them to each other. "Listen, I—"

"I need more time," he said. "I'm not ready to let you go. I think there are things we ought to talk about."

"Yes." She swallowed her relief and swayed toward him a little.

He pulled her the rest of the way. His gaze dropped to her lips. She let her eyes drift closed in anticipation.

His mouth touched hers. Her heart gave a slow thud in her chest. His masculinity flooded her senses, the warmth of his lips on hers making her melt. She opened for him, wanting more, wanting him. He kissed her passionately, deep and long. Odd how she could feel neither the wind nor the rain. She could barely remember where they were by the time a tap on her shoulder interrupted.

A second passed before she pulled away and

could focus on the people around them. Anita, Sam and Carly were looking at them with smiles that stretched from ear to ear.

"Didn't mean to interrupt." Anita grinned the widest.

Cal drew up an eyebrow.

"Get a room," Sam said.

Carly pointed at herself, then at the other two. "Bridesmaids. It's a deal breaker," she told Cal.

Gina winced, but he took her friends in stride. "I took that for granted from the beginning. Ladies, it would be an honor," he said with his most charming smile.

The air got caught in her lungs.

But she didn't have time to think about whether he was serious or just rolling with the joke. The others jumped her with their "Are you okay?" and "We were so worried." They were hugging her for all they were worth, demanding details about everything that had transpired since they had departed.

Complete acceptance.

They knew what she'd done, why she'd been in prison, although not the details. But, oddly, they didn't seem to hold that against her. She was accepted and forgiven. She glanced at Cal. Same there.

And then something shifted inside her. Cal had been right. It was time she forgave herself. She blinked away the tears that clouded her vision all of a sudden.

"You okay?" Sam asked.

"Couldn't be better." Felt ten pounds lighter, for sure.

"What are you doing in the jungle?" Gina asked.

"Looking for you, you—" The sound of gunfire coming from the bay cut Sam off.

"Looks like things are not as secure as they thought," Carly said and threw her a challenging look. "You two lovebirds coming back with us to kick some terrorist butt?"

"I know why you're in a hurry. I bet Nick is here," Gina retorted.

Carly grinned, not bothering to deny it.

Gina smiled back. They were fighting the good fight. They were on the right side. She didn't have to look at Cal to know the answer. "You bet."

"No regrets?" Gina asked.

"None," Cal said, and from the look on his face he meant it. "You were right. Loyalty is tricky. A person has to be loyal to the right people, to the right cause."

She nodded and leaned against the railing, looked out at the endless ocean. "I can't believe you got the yacht."

The cyclone had cleared out as rapidly as it had

descended on the island. The Army boats that had taken them through the zone controlled by pirates had left them now that they were in safe waters. They were alone and out of danger. Hadn't he promised something if such an occasion ever presented itself? The thought was enough to send tingles down her spine.

"They owed me a favor." He moved closer, his gaze on her face, heat swirling in his eyes. "I turned on the autopilot. We have a couple of hours before we get near Acapulco and I have to take over again."

She really hoped he had the same plan for those hours as she did.

He took her hands. "Maybe we should remove ourselves from the sun."

A very sensible suggestion. "Definitely." She followed him toward the cabin, turned out in cherrywood and luxury fabrics, the finest cabinetry work anywhere. The place was spacious as far as boat cabins went but still pretty tight quarters. The sprawling bed took up most of the space.

She sat on the silk bedcover. There wasn't really any other place to go. The room was charged with awareness between them.

"Can I get you a drink?"

She drew up an eyebrow. "Let me guess—you drink martinis."

"Not a great fan, actually. Given a choice, I prefer gin and tonic."

"How very un-Bondish of you. Soda would be fine."

He poured and handed her the crystal glass. "There's another difference between me and Mr. Bond," he said.

"You don't have a souped-up car waiting for us?" she guessed. "It's okay. I'll live with the disappointment."

"Well, of course I have that. I'm a guy. It was my number one priority when I made my first million." His grin faded, his expression turning serious. "But now I want you and only you. Very—how did you say?—un-Bondish. I think he prefers to flitter from woman to woman."

Her heart expanded. "That will considerably extend your life expectancy. I don't do flitterers. I'm Italian-American. We can be a little fierce when it comes to things like that."

He sat on the bed next to her and pulled her onto his lap. He was smiling again, looking pleased as all get-out as he leaned in to kiss her, giving ample demonstration that under all that cool and smooth British demeanor, he wasn't a stranger to fierce.

His hands stole under her shirt, and pleasure skittered across her skin as his palm glided upward.

"I want to spend some serious time with you," he said when he pulled away. "I know it's kind of sudden, but I want you to factor that into your plans when you sit down to figure out what you want to do next."

Her heart thundered. "Consider it figured," she murmured and returned her lips to his.

He dragged his thumb across the undersides of her breasts, making heat pool inside her. It was a little frightening how he could undo her with a look, with a touch, how he could make her body crazy for him.

She stole her hands up his chest, over the wide pane of muscles. He had an incredible body. All in all, he was an incredible man.

His palms moved higher until they covered her aching nipples. The friction sent moisture to the vee of her thighs.

"Hot here," he said between kisses.

"Too much clothing." She helped him out of his shirt as he helped her out of hers.

"You're breathtaking." He caressed her.

Maybe she was being superficial, but she couldn't tear her gaze away from his chest. "Not bad yourself." She outlined his pectoral muscles.

He sucked in a breath when she got to his flat, hard nipples. She leaned forward and kissed first one, then the other.

He laid her gently on the bed, pushed her bikini top out of the way and returned the favor. When he gently began to suckle an engorged tip, she nearly came off the bed with the exquisite sensation.

Then he did some twirly thing.

"What was that?" she asked when she regained her breath.

"Trying to learn what you like." He applied pressure to the nipple between his lips.

"So far, so good," she said when she could talk again.

"I believe in slow, careful learning. One's studies should always be deliberate."

"Is that the English method?" She sighed as he nibbled his way up her neck. "I like it."

"I'm a thorough sort of chap."

"Commendable—" She forgot whatever else she was about to say when his hand slipped inside her shorts. "I…it's been a while." She rode the building pressure, feeling none of the slow-careful thing he seemed to possess. She was in more of a quick-and-reckless frame of mind. Cultural differences, she supposed.

He flicked the button open and dragged the shorts down over her feet, then let them drop to the floor. She was naked save her bikini bottom.

"And finally the naughty bits," he said with a sly look and hooked a finger into the waistband.

Naughty bits? She hated the silly grin she knew must be sitting on her face. She was just going to have to get over it. Because she liked the way he handled her naughty bits. She liked it a lot.

His naughty bits were straining the zipper of his fly. She eased their plight by tugging the zipper down. That didn't seem enough. She peeled his pants over his hips and down his legs. Now they were even. And…oh, my.

Her eyes, which had gone wide at the sight of him, floated closed the next second as he invaded her body with a long finger, parting her flesh, eliciting waves of pleasure. She didn't notice when the bikini bottoms disappeared. The boxer shorts vanished just as miraculously.

He held her gaze, filling her slowly, stretching her, pushing her higher and higher onto some imaginary cliff of pleasure. He barely got all the way when she reached the peak and soared, her muscles pulsating around him.

He gave her a very rakish and satisfied smile.

"Hey, I'm part of the fast-food generation, attention deficit and whatever. I don't think I should be expected to know slow." Then she grew oddly embarrassed for a second. "I didn't mean to rush to the end."

He began to move with a deliberate, tantalizing pace. "What end? We've barely started."

And then he proved it to her.

An hour later, when they lay sated in each other's arms, she said, "It hasn't… Is it like this for others? I've never… It was like in the movies. Did you use some secret trick? Some British thing?"

He gathered her close and grinned at her. "It's a love thing, luv," he said.

Epilogue

"Is this an American thing?" Cal held up the fifth pair of handcuffs they'd gotten as a wedding present.

"It's a cop thing." Gina took them away from him. A couple of her ex-colleagues had attended the wedding.

"Not that I'm complaining."

She raised an eyebrow but couldn't help a smile. "We could always return them."

"Absolutely not, Mrs. Spencer. That would be rude. You should know by now that us Brits are unfailingly polite," he said with mock severity.

Guests whirled around them in the grand ballroom at the Berkley in London. Her sisters were on the dance floor, as were Anita, Carly and Sam, the sisters of her heart. Her ex-teammates were in various stages of engagement and battling prewedding nerves themselves. Their records had been cleared and now they could all focus on the future.

All four of them had found new lives, new loves, new hope. Gina's hand slid to her belly, where something else new was growing day by day. Cal's arm came around her and he put a hand over hers, over their unborn child.

She smiled up at him.

Once, she had believed that the dangerous mission she'd been recruited to was *Mission: Impossible*. She knew better now. It had been *Mission: Redemption* for all of them.

* * * * *

Keep reading for an exclusive extract from

High-Stakes Honeymoon
by RaeAnne Thayne,

out in July 2008 from
Mills & Boon® Intrigue.

High-Stakes Honeymoon
by RaeAnne Thayne

Olivia sighed, gazing out at the ripple of waves as she tried to drum up a little enthusiasm for the holiday that stretched ahead of her like the vast, undulating surface of the Pacific. She'd been here less than twenty-four hours and had nine more days to go, and at this point she was just about ready to pack up her suitcases and catch the next puddle jumper she could find back to the States.

She was bored and lonely and just plain miserable.

Maybe she should have invited one of her girlfriends to come along for company. Or better yet, she should have just eaten the cost of the plane tickets and stayed back in Fort Worth.

But then she would have had to face the questions and the sympathetic—and not so sympathetic—looks and the resigned disappointment she was entirely too accustomed to seeing in her father's eyes.

No, this way was better. If nothing else, ten days in another country would give her a little time and distance to handle the bitter betrayal of knowing that even in this, Wallace Lambert wouldn't stand behind her. Her father sided with his golden boy, his groomed successor, and couldn't seem to understand why she might possibly object to her fiancé cheating on her with another woman two weeks before their wedding.

It was apparently entirely unreasonable of her to expect a few basic courtesies—minor little things like fidelity and trust—from the man who claimed to adore her and worship the ground she walked on.

Who knew?

The sun slipped further into the water and she

sighed again, angry at herself. So much for her promise that she wouldn't brood about Bradley or her father.

This was her honeymoon and she planned to enjoy herself, damn them both. She could survive nine more days in paradise, in the company of macaws and howler monkeys, iguanas and even a sloth—not to mention her host, whom she had yet to encounter.

James Rafferty, whom she was meeting later for dinner, had built his fortune through online gambling and he had created an exclusive paradise here completely off the grid—no power except through generators, water from wells on the property. Even her cell phone didn't work here.

Nine days without distractions ought to be long enough for her to figure out what she was going to do with the rest of her life. She was twenty-six years old and it was high time she shoved everybody else out of the driver's seat so she could start picking her own direction.

Some kind of animal screamed suddenly, a high, disconcerting sound, and Olivia jumped, suddenly uneasy to realize she was alone down here on the beach.

There were jaguars in this part of the Osa Peninsula, she had read in the guidebook. Jaguars and pumas and who knew what else. A big cat could suddenly spring out of the jungle and drag her into the trees, and no one in the world would ever know what happened to her.

That would certainly be a fitting end to what had to be the world's worst honeymoon.

She shivered and quickly gathered up her things, shaking the sand out of her towel and tossing her sunglasses and paperback into her beach bag along with her cell phone that she couldn't quite sever herself from, despite its uselessness here.

No worries, she told herself. She seemed to remember jaguars hunted at night and it was still a half hour to full dark. Anyway, she had a hard time believing James Rafferty would allow wild predators such as that to roam free on his vast estate.

Still, she wasn't at all sure she could find her way back to her bungalow in the dark, and she needed to shower off the sand and sunscreen and change for dinner.

She had waited too long to return, she quickly discovered. She would have thought the dying rays of the sun would provide enough light for her to make her way back to her bungalow, fifty yards or so from the beach up a moderate incline. But the trail moved through heavy growth, feathery ferns and flowering shrubs and thick trees with vines roped throughout.

What had seemed lovely and exotic on her way down to the beach suddenly seemed darker, almost menacing, in the dusk.

Something rustled in the thick undergrowth to her left. She swallowed a gasp and picked up her pace, those jaguars prowling through her head again.

Next time she would watch the sunset from the comfort of her own little front porch, she decided nervously. Of course, from what the taciturn housekeeper who had brought her food earlier said, this dry sunset was an anomaly this time of year, given the daily rains.

Wasn't it just like Bradley to book their honeymoon destination without any thought that they were arriving in the worst month of the rainy season. She would probably be stuck in her bungalow the entire nine days.

Still grumbling under her breath, she made it only a few more feet before a dark shape suddenly lurched out of the gathering darkness. She uttered a small shriek of surprise and barely managed to keep her footing.

In the fading light, she could only make out a stranger looming over her, dark and menacing. Something long and lethal gleamed silver in the fading light, and a strangled scream escaped her.

He held a machete, a wickedly sharp one, and she gazed at it, riveted like a bug watching a frog's tongue flicking toward it. She couldn't seem to look away as it gleamed in the last fading rays of the sun.

She was going to die alone on her honeymoon in a foreign country in a bikini that showed just how lousy she was at keeping up with her Pilates.

Her only consolation was that the stranger seemed just as surprised to see her. She supposed someone with rape on his mind probably wouldn't waste time staring at her as if she were some kind of freakish sea creature.

Come on. The bikini wasn't *that* bad.

She opened her mouth to say something—she wasn't quite sure what—but before she could come up with anything, he gave a quick look around, then grabbed her from behind, shoving the hand not holding the machete against her mouth.